# *"I should retreat now before I make any more of an idiot of myself—"*

"No, don't," Tess said, grabbing Eli's hand, just to keep him from leaving. Eli grabbed hers back, then tugged her to him, his eyes touching hers for about half a second—barely long enough for a "Wha—?" to skate through her brain—and lowered his mouth to hers.

She tensed, then thought, *What the hell?* and kissed him back, no grappling involved, no body parts touching except lips, the merest suggestion of tongue, their linked hands…and Eli's strong, rough fingers on the nape of her neck. Whee, doggie. She kissed him back, and he kissed her back more, and basically she turned into one big quivering mass of goo.

Just from his lips touching hers? Holy cow.

When it was over—much too soon—Eli chuckled again, sheepish, and Tess had to grab the railing, she was quivering so badly.

"This isn't working, is it?" he said, and Tess barked out a laugh.

"Our staying out of each other's way? No. Apparently not…"

Dear Reader,

Those of you familiar with the previous two books in my WED IN THE WEST series have already met Tess Montoya, the spunky, irreverent, and generous-hearted gal whose husband was stationed in Iraq. And all during the telling of those two stories, I thought for sure I knew what Tess's story was going to be. Turned out I was wrong. Funny, how the Muse likes to play tricks like that.

Oh, I knew hers would be a story about starting over. I just had no idea she'd be starting over with somebody else. Let alone that the somebody else would be her first love.

I also had no idea, when I started, just how hard it was going to be for Tess to learn to trust again…or how much fun it would be to watch Eli Garrett—the aforementioned first love, seen briefly in *Reining in the Rancher*—grow into the stalwart, sweet, there-for-her guy she needs him to be.

It's okay if you swoon a little, I'll understand. ;-)

*Karen*

# A MARRIAGE-MINDED MAN

## *KAREN TEMPLETON*

# SPECIAL EDITION®

Published by Silhouette Books

**America's Publisher of Contemporary Romance**

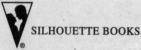

SILHOUETTE BOOKS

ISBN-13: 978-0-373-65476-5

A MARRIAGE-MINDED MAN

PLEASE RECYCLE

THIS PRODUCT IS RECYCLABLE

Recycling programs
for this product may
not exist in your area.

**Books by Karen Templeton**

---

## KAREN TEMPLETON

A Waldenbooks bestselling author and RITA® Award nominee, Karen Templeton is the mother of five sons and living proof that romance and dirty diapers are not mutually exclusive. An Easterner transplanted to Albuquerque, New Mexico, she spends far too much time trying to coax her garden to yield roses and produce something resembling a lawn, all the while fantasizing about a weekend alone with her husband. Or at least an uninterrupted conversation.

She loves to hear from readers, who may reach her by writing c/o Silhouette Books, 233 Broadway, Suite 1001, New York, NY 10279, or online at www.karentempleton.com.

To Jack,
for always being there
even when I'm sure there were times when you wondered
what on earth you'd gotten into!

## Chapter One

Crackly leaves darted out of the old pickup's way as Eli Garrett effortlessly navigated the mountain road, one hand resting lightly on the steering wheel, the other thrumming the dashboard in time to Willie Nelson. Behind him, like backup, ladders and tools and whatnot rattled and rumbled in the truck's bed.

*Good times,* Eli thought as he approached the final, dusk-cloaked curve to his house. He had a check from a thrilled client in his pocket, 007 waiting in his mailbox, and Evangelista Ortega's chicken enchiladas tucked up all nice and cozy in the aluminum tray on the seat beside him. So the late fall evening stretched before him, gloriously free, nothin' to do except hang with Mr. Bond and chow down on the best enchiladas this side of Santa Fe. Maybe in all of New Mexico, he mused, cresting the hill—

"What the hell—!"

He swerved to avoid the small, ghostlike figure who'd popped up out of nowhere, jogging on the wrong damn side of the road. The figure shrieked, then toppled over into a thicket of brush and chamisa, cussing in a mixture of Spanish and English loud enough to blow poor Willie right off the map.

All the junk in the truck bed crashed mightily as Eli jerked up short on the shoulder ahead and jumped out. "I'm sorry, I didn't see you!" he yelled, striding toward the figure, already getting to her feet. "You okay?" In the glow from his taillights, she spun around, glaring, and what was left of Eli's good mood evaporated like smoke in a high wind.

He froze, unsure of his next move. Recognizing him, Teresa Morales—wrong, *Montoya*—stiffened, too, a moment before a dry, caustic laugh sprang from her mouth. Eli relaxed. Some.

"Holy hell, Tess—you trying to give me a heart attack?"

Swiping dirt, dead leaves and chamisa gunk off her butt, Tess shot him The Look of Death. "Yeah, well," she said, "you didn't exactly do my cardiovascular system any favors, either. Crap." Shoving a headband off her short, wavy hair, she plunked back down in the dirt, inspecting an ugly-ass dark slash on her shin. "Am I bleeding? I can't see a damn thing in this light."

"If I look, you promise not to go after me with a blunt object?"

Her eyes flashed to his, then back to the cut. "It's your lucky day—I'm unarmed."

"You sure? That headband looks kinda dangerous—"

"Geez, Eli—just look at my leg, okay?"

Eli squatted beside her, trying not to react to her scent, the same one that used to make his eyes cross as a horny seventeen-year-old. That threatened to short out his brain now. Especially when he yanked up her leg to get a better look and came into contact with all that cool, smooth skin—

"Ow!"

"Sorry," he mumbled. Rubbing the underside of her calf, a little. Noticing she'd recently shaved. Or waxed. Or something. Stubble, the curse of the dark-haired, she'd said. "Yeah, you're bleeding all right. Must've been a branch or something stickin' out, scratched you up pretty good. What in tarnation were you doing runnin' this time of night? And why on earth were you way out here?"

"It was still daylight when I started," she muttered, digging a tissue out of her body-hugging, light-colored jacket. "And I didn't mean to run this far—or even run at all, I'd just gone for a walk—but it sorta got away from me." He noticed her hand trembling as she dabbed at the blood, like most of the fight had gone out of her.

Like a woman still stinging from her recent divorce, maybe?

Eli sighed. "Hold on, I've got paper towels and water in the truck."

Amazingly, she was still there when he returned, her forehead propped on her arms, folded across her knees. Knowing Tess, he'd half expected to see her hobbling down the road, muttering, "Don't need no stinkin' help from no stinkin', stupid ex-boyfriends." He handed her a soaked towel. "Here."

She jerked her head up like she'd forgotten about him, then took the damp towel and pressed it to the wound, clearly holding back a wince. A single tear dribbled down her cheek, looking like blood itself in the red glow. She shouldered it away.

"You okay?"

"I'm fine," she snapped, then released a breath, her mouth set. "Really," she said, more softly, and it was everything he could do not to call her on the obvious lie.

Eli sat back on his haunches, trying to reconcile what he saw in front of him with both the carefree sixteen-year-old girl his hormone-crazed younger self had been crazy in love with and the sharp, confident businesswoman she'd become over the past few years. Or so he'd heard, since they'd barely exchanged ten words since Eli's Big Screwup.

Even so, in a town like Tierra Rosa you could go for years without talking to somebody and still know every detail of their lives. Either you'd overhear something, or some kind soul would fill you in, or you'd notice things with your own two eyes. Things you kept to yourself, no matter how much they might be killing you inside.

"Where's the kids?" he asked, exchanging the bloodied towel for a clean one.

"In Albuquerque. With their father," Tess said through a grimace. She glanced at him, just long enough for him to catch the anger-tinged shadows in her eyes, then back at her leg, pressing the towel to the wound. "Yesterday would have been our ninth anniversary."

"Sorry."

She shrugged. Lifted the towel. "You think it's stopped?"

"Can't really tell in the dark. Can you walk?"

"Of course I can walk," she said, rising and putting her weight on her foot. Doing the stoic thing.

"Come on, I'll take you back to my place and get you patched up."

Clearly gritting her teeth, Tess took another step. Swore under her breath. "How about you take me home instead?"

"Because something tells me you shouldn't be alone right now."

Even in the dark, he felt the full force of her glare. Caught the pain behind it, too. And not just because of her leg. "And I don't recall asking for your input. If you don't want to give me a lift, I'll get back on my own steam."

"Before next Sunday?"

The glare intensified. Eli almost laughed. "Tell you what—how about we go back to my place and get the dirt cleaned out of that scratch, *then* I'll take you home?" When she still hesitated, he said, "Might even rustle up a slug of whiskey from somewhere."

"Why? In case you need to amputate?"

"Never hurts to be prepared."

Muttering something about "damn Boy Scouts," Tess started for the truck. Eli tried to put his arm around her waist, got his hand smacked for the trouble. Of course, she then limped the ten feet to the passenger-side door, leaning against the extended cab for dear life while Eli shifted the enchiladas so she'd have some place to sit. Once settled in her seat, however, she emitted a sound that was half sigh, half moan.

"Those Eva's enchiladas?" she asked.

"They are." Huh. "When's the last time you ate?"

Tess erased the frown before—she thought—Eli noticed it. "A while ago."

Thinking, *Women, sheesh*, Eli slammed shut her door and walked around the truck's hood. Got in. "I got no problem sharing."

"That's okay, I'm fine."

Shaking his head, he pulled back out onto the road. "Your stomach might take issue with you on that."

Tess crossed her arms over her loudly rumbling middle. "There's food at home."

Eli decided to quit while he still had all his crucial body parts.

It didn't take but a couple of minutes to get to his place, a nondescript pseudo-adobe number he'd bought some time ago, close to a much larger building that housed the family woodworking and cabinetry business, which in turn was maybe fifty yards away from his parents' house. Award-worthy? God, no. Affordable and convenient? You bet.

Tess slid out of the truck on her own steam—big surprise,

there—taking a second to either get her bearings or scrutinize the house. Maybe both.

"Hard to get the full effect in the dark," he said, carting the enchiladas past her, figuring she'd hobble behind when she was ready.

"I'm sure," she muttered. Hobbling along behind.

Eventually she made it inside the house. "Huh," she said, although to the open space—the result of his knocking out a bunch of non-load-bearing walls after he'd first bought the place—or the lack of Clueless Bachelor clutter, he couldn't say.

"Yeah, good thing the maid came today," he said, carting the enchiladas to the kitchen.

"Maid?"

After putting the tray on the counter, Eli shrugged out of his denim jacket. "No, Tess, no maid. Not that I'm suggesting you eat off the floor, but I do know how to wash a dish and take out the garbage."

"Oh, I…" She blew out a sigh, then pointed to her wound. "Triage?"

"Right straight through, on your right. First-aid kit's under the sink. I take it you don't need my help?"

"No," she said, hobbling off. Ten seconds later, he heard a shriek. Eli hotfooted it to the bathroom to find Tess gawking at her reflection in the medicine chest mirror. "How come you didn't tell me I have half the national forest in my hair?" she asked, plucking at twigs and chamisa fluff and stuff, and in the light he could see that twelve years and a couple of kids had added a few not-unwelcome pounds here and there.

"It was dark," he said. "Couldn't tell." He leaned one palm against the doorjamb, appreciating the view. "Don't think I've ever seen you with short hair."

Her eyes cut to his for barely a second before veering back to the mirror. "Got tired of taking care of it long," she said

softly, bitterly, finger-combing most of the chamisa gunk out
of it, sending the yellow bits floating all over his bathroom.

*Don't get sucked in, don't get—*

"Looks good," he said, then walked away and left her to it.

Tess braced herself against his sink—far cleaner than she
would have expected, nothing on it except a cup and a razor—
willing her heart to settle down.

What on earth had she been thinking, not turning back
long before she'd gotten so far from her own house? She
supposed that had been the whole point, that she'd wanted to
run away. From everything. Not forever, just for a little while.
But to end up in Eli Garrett's bathroom?

Beyond weird.

If they'd seen each other a half dozen times since their
breakup, she'd be surprised. It wasn't anything deliberate,
exactly, even if their parting had been, well, pretty bad. In ret-
rospect, chasing him down Main Street with a sponge mop
had probably been a bit over the top. Not that she would have
inflicted any lasting damage—she didn't think—even if
there'd been the slightest chance of catching up with those
long legs of his. But for heaven's sake, it wasn't like she still
had any feelings for the guy. Not after a dozen years and a
couple of kids and a marriage blowing up in her face—

Sighing, Tess hauled out the first-aid kit, getting her first
good look at her boo-boo. Eww. She'd hardly be crippled for
life, but miniskirts had just been crossed off the list for the
near future.

She banged down the toilet seat and sank onto it, dampen-
ing a gauze pad with antiseptic before tentatively touching it
to the wound. She hissed, then swore, as hot tears bit at her
eyes—from the pain, yes, but more from a sudden surge of
anger and frustration, topped with a leftover jalapeño or two

of grief. All that time, petrified of losing Ricky to something she didn't even fully understand, only to discover she'd lost him anyway.

Yeah, there was some sick irony for you.

The grief, Tess could handle. Had handled, for the most part. People change, marriages die, let's move on. The anger, however…this was new. The anger was what had propelled her out the door two hours ago, fueled a run that had lasted far longer than it should have, made her take risks she would have never normally taken.

The anger frightened her because she didn't know its limits. What it would do. What it would make *her* do.

She glopped on some antibiotic ointment, then bandaged the scrape. Already, the shock of the fall was wearing off. When she stood this time, her leg seemed more inclined to do its job. The kit shoved back underneath Eli's sink, she made her way to the front room, a living/dining combo all rustic and woodsy—and surprisingly homey—with its wooden floor and paneling, the dark beams running the length of the white ceiling. The decorating style was strictly Early Parental Cast Offs—she thought she recognized the old beige corduroy sofa—but mercifully devoid of ancient pizza boxes and beer cans.

One might not even think a bachelor lived here at all, had it not been for the two solid shelves of video game cases and the corresponding jumble of consoles under, beside and around the boxy, '90s-issue TV squatting in the entertainment center like a bloated rhinoceros.

"So what's the prognosis?" Eli called from the dining nook, which is when she noticed not only that he'd set the table for two, but the man who'd set that table.

Taller. More solid. Curly, light brown hair still too long, the Henley T-shirt still too loose, the jeans still ragged. The person wearing them still too damn sure of himself for his own good. And—much as it pained her to admit it—for hers.

Her hands stuffed in her jacket front pocket, Tess shrugged, reminding herself the sexually predatory divorcée was *such* a cliché. "No worries on that amputation thing. Um…what's this?"

"Dinner," he said, flashing her the dimpled grin that had been her undoing so long ago. Ducking the not-half-bad wrought-iron chandelier over the table, he set down a plate of enchiladas, then another, like Enrique used to once upon a time, when they were first married and the future beckoned, unblemished and secure.

The anger flared. "I thought I said—"

"I know what you said," Eli said mildly, although there was nothing mild about the way he was looking at her. *Don't do that!* she wanted to yell, even as longing—hot and thick and syrupy— welled inside her to mix with the anger. Since, you know, he looked at pretty much every female in the county like that—

"I've also been working my butt off all day," he continued, still watching her, and her eyes latched onto his mouth, and another memory flashed, of what good a kisser he'd been, and she realized she was an inch away from pity party status, which only made her madder—

"And you live clear on the other side of town. So I'm gonna eat before I take you home, if it's all the same to you. And since my mama taught me it's rude to eat in front of people without offering to share…" He gestured toward the plate on the far side of the table. "You may as well join me."

Staring at the table, Tess removed one hand from its cocoon to jerk her hair behind her ear—a habit left over from when she'd still had hair. For some reason, this set the anger loose all over again. Not a single, neatly defined emotion or reaction to any one particular thing, but a whole damn herd of pissed-off thoughts, stampeding through her brain and soul and body—

"Tess?"

Eli'd said her name so softly it took a moment to register. "It's okay," he said gently when she jerked her gaze to his, and her eyes burned, partly because it wasn't true—at all— and partly because it felt so strange, somebody reassuring *her,* a job that had been hers for as long as she could remember. His hands resting lightly along the top of one of the high-backed wooden chairs, his gaze was warm and steady and completely unthreatening. Not at all what she'd thought she'd seen earlier.

Yeah, like that was a step in the right direction.

Only because she was starving, and because her options at home began and ended with frozen pizza, she sighed out a "Fine," her leg only hurting a little as she crossed to the table, plopping into the chair he held out for her. She thought she might've caught a smile before Eli turned to the refrigerator, a white, no-nonsense old-timer that wobbled slightly when he opened the door. "What would you like to drink? I got tea, Coke, water—"

"What happened to the booze offer?"

He turned, eyes sparkling, dimples dimpling, and wasn't she *thrilled* to notice they were both far more deadly now than they had been a dozen years ago? And they'd been pretty damn deadly then. "Somehow I'm thinking whiskey on an empty stomach isn't the best idea."

And *she* was thinking she'd never get through the next twenty minutes without something to dull her senses. Especially those prone to reacting to cocky smiles from sexy old boyfriends with baaaaad reputations. "Beer, then? Unless you don't have any."

"Oh, I've got some, but—"

"Then hand her over." At Eli's dubious—and annoyingly protective—look, she sighed. "I can hold a single beer, Eli."

Never mind the nasty little voice whispering that, actually, no, she couldn't, which was why she rarely drank. "Especially if I'm eating."

The voice sniggered.

Oh, for crying out loud—so what if she got a little buzz on? She somehow doubted the world would implode. But dammit, she thought as she watched Eli pour out a can of Bud into a tall glass—which he rinsed out first—she'd been responsible for everyone and everything for so, *so* long, what was one little old beer in the scheme of things? And besides—

"And besides—" Her hands fisted on the table, she looked him square in the eye. "This is weird, okay? Me being here with you, in your house. What with all the other weirdnesses going on in my life…"

"Got it." Eli handed her the beer, then sat with his own, and he was all big and solid and manly and such, and she remembered that baaaad reputation of his.

"Don't *you* think this is weird?" she asked, shivering a little.

"Heck, yeah," he said, lifting his glass to her. Spearing her with those eerie light brown eyes. Almost gold. Kinda the same color as his hair. The too-long hair half covering his ears, glossy in the chandelier's light, all those hard-edged features at odds with those soft, soft curls—

Tess tipped back her glass; three gulps later, it was half-gone—

"Hey," she said when Eli grabbed it from her. "Give that back."

"Not until you eat something," he said, tucking into his own food while holding her glass just out of reach, the creep. Only after Tess downed several bites and her eyes were streaming from the chili did Eli take pity on her and return her drink. Her mouth on fire, she finished it off. The belch just kind of escaped.

"Whoa," Eli said. Grinning. Tess blinked, thinking she

could practically see the pheromones rising from his warm skin. Like ghosts from a graveyard on Halloween.

*And you know this is only because every time you see Ricky you go a little crazy. Has nothing to do with Eli.*

"You know, these are almost as good as mine," she said, jabbing her fork at the enchiladas. Which were beginning to get a little blurry.

"No way," Eli said, forking in a huge mouthful. "Nobody makes enchiladas better'n Evangelista."

"Oh, and you would know this how? I love Eva with all my heart, but my grandmother's recipe… People have been known to kill for her enchiladas."

"Seriously?"

"Okay, not really. But close." Tess took another bite. Then burped again. And frowned at her glass. "S'empty."

Laughing, Eli stood, pulling a pitcher from the fridge. "How 'bout some tea now?"

"Hell, no. I can have tea at home." She held out her glass, suddenly fascinated with the way it sparkled in the light from the chandelier. "Hit me with another Bud, bud." She giggled. And hiccupped.

Eli got a funny look on his face. "You sure?"

She rolled her eyes. They felt a little loose. "Not driving, I'm good. Oh, come on—have pity on the poor divorcée, huh? What's the worst that can happen?"

"You get bombed and puke all over my rug?"

Tess shook her head. Decided maybe she shouldn't do that again. "I didn't even throw up when I was pregnant," she said, which made her sad, thinking about her babies and how much she loved them and how hard it was when they were off with their father, even though that only happened maybe once a month, if that, and that here she was, sitting in Eli Garrett's kitchen, drinking his beer and not even thinking about them. Except she was, because she was *always* thinking about her babies.

She thought maybe she was getting a little…confused.

Nothing another beer couldn't fix, right?

"Please," she said, and Eli took her glass, pouring another beer into it, God bless his baaaaad self.

"Need any help?" Eli heard Tess ask when he went to clear the table shortly after they'd finished their meal.

"Nope. All under control. Soon as I give 'em a rinse, I'll run you home. If you're ready."

She gave him a slightly guarded smile, then nodded. "Sure thing," she said, getting to her feet. More or less steadily, he was relieved to note. Not that she was exactly sober—*feeling no pain* was the phrase that came to mind—but thankfully she'd stopped well short of stupid drunk. Eli'd been with his share of stupid drunk women over the years; whatever amusement he'd at one time found in those sorts of shenanigans had long since faded. And besides, Tess getting plastered…just didn't seem right.

In any case, he got the feeling the beer had only been an excuse to let go—which something told him she hadn't done in a very long while. Not that she'd gone all maudlin on him or anything; mostly, they talked about her kids, Miguel and Julia—pronounced with an *H* instead of a *J*— and his recently married and very much younger brother, Jesse, and his wife, Rachel, how they were dealing with being new parents, stuff like that. In fact, whenever Eli'd tried to steer the conversation in Tess's direction, she'd steer it right back.

Because, okay, he was curious about what had happened between her and Enrique, who'd been deployed overseas for most of their marriage. Maybe more than curious—he'd watched his older brother, Silas, go through a nasty divorce, knew how hard it was. Especially on the good ones. Like his brother. Or Tess.

Still, the protective feelings boiling up inside him went way beyond your garden-variety gee-I-hope-she's-okay concern. What did it matter to him whether she got drunk or not? Or made a fool of herself?

So why, as he stood at the sink, half watching her walk into his living room with her hands tucked into her jacket's front pouch, did he feel compelled to make sure she wasn't gonna keel over or anything?

"Everything okay in there?" he called over.

Tess nodded. A little too vigorously. "I like what you've done here."

Stacking the plates in the dishwasher, he laughed. "I think 'done' might be overstating it. Unless you consider shoving around a bunch of castoffs and thrift store junk so I can walk through the room without injuring myself 'done.'"

"It's…" She gave him a puzzled look over her shoulder. "You."

"Lot to be said for not having to consider anybody else's opinion." The dishwasher shut, he was about to say, "Ready?" when she spun around and collapsed into the couch, an old beige corduroy number that had been in his parents' family room. The fluff was worn off in some places, and the cushions sagged from being crushed by a whole bunch of butts over the years, but it was still comfortable as hell—

"What's wrong?" he said when Tess leaned into the cushions, her eyes closed.

"Probably shouldn't've done that spinning thing."

"You gonna be sick?"

She laughed softly. "Told you. I don't do that."

"Not even when you get stomach flu?"

"Nope. And by the way, technically that's not the flu."

"Technically, I don't much care what it's called. And how do you not throw up?"

"Sheer willpower," she said, except the words seemed a little frayed around the edges. Eli crossed his arms, trying not to think how soft and vulnerable she looked, all sunk into those deep cushions with her eyes closed like that. "Comfy?"

"As comfy as one can be when your brain's on the puree setting."

"So you *are* drunk."

"Maybe. A little." Finally, she opened her eyes, frowning at him. "I didn't expect you to be…nice."

Eli frowned. "I'm always nice—"

"I mean *really* nice."

"What that's supposed to mean?"

"I'm not entirely sure." Tess snuggled farther into the corner of the sofa, letting out a shriek when the mass of fur that owned the place jumped up onto the sofa arm beside her. "Dear God—what's that?"

"A cat. What's it look like?"

"Something from a '50s horror movie. After the radiation experiment went horribly wrong. Wait—" She shifted her frown to Eli. "You have a cat?"

"Got a problem with that?"

"Geez, touchy much?" she said, then looked at the cat again. Leaning back a little. "He's bigger than my two-year-old."

"She. And *big* is a definite advantage when you live in the woods. Chased a bear up a tree once."

"You're kidding."

"Wanna see the video?"

"No, I'll take your word for it. Does she have a name?"

She would have to ask. Warmth prickled his cheeks. "Maybelline."

Tess's wide-eyed gaze flew to his; a moment later, she snorted out a very unladylike laugh. "You're not serious."

"I didn't name her, okay? Some lady we were working for, it had been her mother's cat, only the old lady died and her daughter was allergic. Damn thing glommed on to me from the moment I walked into her house, so she asked me if I wanted her."

"And you actually said yes."

"She'd already asked, like, ten people. It was me or the pound. Anyway, look at that face—how could I say no to that face?"

Another laugh. "And you actually call her Maybelline?"

"Actually, I call her Belly. For obvious reasons."

Sitting on the arm of the sofa and purring loud enough to rattle skulls in a five-mile radius, Belly shot an offended look in Eli's direction, although with one eye partly closed and her snaggleteeth on full display the effect was kinda lost. One ear was half–bitten off—Eli didn't want to know what she'd tangled with, or what condition she'd left the other guy in—and it'd been a while since she'd let him brush out the knots in her fur. He supposed maybe she didn't give the best first impression.

Now, sensing some lovin' in the offing, she jumped down and trotted over to Eli, her saggy belly swaying from side to side. In one swipe, Belly coated the bottom of his jeans with a half inch of cat fur. Eli scooped her up to roughly scratch under her chin, getting her motor going full throttle. Cat did love her chin rubs.

"You. With a cat. Unbelievable." Tess grinned, for a second looking almost like the girl he used to know. A moment later, though, she swiped the red Netflix envelope off the end table next to her, slipping out the sleeved disk. "Bond, huh?" she said, and Eli thought, *Why are you still here?*

Because she was making him feel maybe not so protective, which was in turn making him twitchy. He scratched the cat harder.

"Not just Bond. Craig's Bond."

"I'm a Brosnan girl, myself."

"Get out." *Please.*

"What can I say?" she said, pushing herself to her feet. "I like suave…oh, hell—"

Cat went flying when Eli lunged forward to catch Tess as her knees buckled. She molded herself to his chest—what the hell?—only to immediately shove away again, shaking her head. Good call.

"You need to sit," he said, trying to make her sit.

"I don't need to sit. I'm fine, I'm—"

Tears bloomed in her eyes before she pushed past him to the door. Except she wobbled again, crashing into an armchair.

"For God's sake, Tess—!"

She wheeled on him. "Do you know how long it's been since I've watched a movie with another adult?"

That *thud* he heard in his head would be any hope of getting her out of his house before one of them did something stupid. Because clearly whatever she'd been keeping locked up inside her was only now lurching to the surface. And, since she was there to begin with at his insistence, dumping her now probably wouldn't be cool.

Yeah, this would be a good time for the evil, scum-sucking side of his personality to kick in. If he'd had one. "You're more than welcome to stay and watch—"

"That's not the point!" Tess cried, charging him. Flailing a bit. "The point is…" She stopped, shaking her head, looking a little wild-eyed. "The point is, that there is no point! To any of it!"

She'd started pacing his living room like she was fixing to lift off any moment. Maybe not the best time to interrupt the flow.

"You know what I felt when Ricky said he wanted a divorce? *Relief.* That I could finally stop holding my breath, because it was *over.* He was officially no longer my responsibility! No more lying awake at night, worrying…no more wondering when he'd be home, if he'd even make it home…no more going around with a fake smile plastered across my face, pretending that everything was just hunky-dory when all I wanted to do was hit something, some*body,* only to find out he'd fallen out of love with me! All that worrying for nothing, Eli! *Nothing!*"

She closed in on him, fists raised; although she couldn't have hurt him if she tried, Eli grabbed her wrists, then wrapped his arms around her, holding her tight as all hell broke loose, as she railed against her husband for leaving her and the kids for months on end, for coming back from Iraq only to leave her for good. Then, somehow, they were on the couch, and he was holding her in his lap—just trying to comfort her, stop the emotional hemorrhage—when he all of a sudden realized they were kissing, seriously kissing with tongue and everything, and while on one level he was enjoying it and all, in the back of his mind he thought, *Dude— seriously messed up.*

And wasn't now a helluva time for the growing-up thing to kick in?

So he wrenched their mouths apart and said, "This is just you being drunk and upset," and she said, "Yeah, so?" and planted another one on him, and blood rushed hither and yon, doing what rushing blood will do, and it occurred to him watching movies wasn't all Tess hadn't done with another adult in a long time.

Especially when she mumbled, "*Please* tell me you've got condoms."

## Chapter Two

With more regret than the world would ever know, Eli put some distance—not enough, but some—between him and the woman currently responsible for an erection so hard his ears were ringing.

"Honey—you don't really want this."

Her answer to that was to unzip her running suit top and struggle out of it, tossing it over her shoulder, her exercise bra no match for her nipples' attempts to punch right through the stretchy fabric. "And if you don't touch my breasts within the next two seconds, I may have to kill you." When Eli shook his head, she clamped her hands around his face and stared him right in the eye. "They *hurt*, Eli. *I* hurt—"

"And you're going to hurt ten times worse if we do this." She smacked his shoulder. "What the hell—?"

"Since when do you become honorable?" she said, smacking him again, although her hundred pounds—if that—were barely gonna make an impression on his one-eighty. "Geez, Eli—you sleep with anything with hooters! So how come you choose *now* to rustle up some scruples?"

She gasped when he grabbed her wrists, jerking her into silence. Bringing their faces within kissing distance again, he ground out, "I do not, and never have, slept with every woman who came on to me. And I sure as hell am not gonna take advantage of somebody who's only looking for a little stress relief!"

Her swollen mouth set, Tess locked gazes with him for a long moment, then reached up and took off her bra. Eli groaned. And stared. What? Like he was gonna look away? Then he frowned.

"They're bigger."

"Yeah, two kids'll do that. So. You got condoms or what?"

"Yeah, I got condoms. But you hate me."

That seemed to sober her for a moment. Then, smiling, she thrust her hands through his hair and kissed him again, open-mouthed and hot and slow and thorough, and his scruples packed up their little bags and began to shuffle off, sighing. Day-um, the woman could kiss. Then she finally came up for air, pressed her forehead to his and ground certain eager body parts to his equally eager body parts and said, panting, "I'm drunk and mad and horny and half-naked. Could you please just shut up and go with the flow here?" And it occurred to him that he'd hurt her a lot more by rejecting her than simply doing what she wanted.

At least, that's the story he was going with.

So he wound her more tightly around him and stood, carrying her into the bedroom, not even bothering to pull back the covers before he dropped her on the bed and ripped off her bicycle shorts and cotton panties, realizing he was more than a little pissed off himself as he stripped off his own clothes and yanked open the dresser drawer.

"So, you want me to just—"

"Yes," she hissed, getting to her knees to yank him onto the bed. Snatching the condom out of his hand, she shoved him on his back, straddling him, sheathing him. A moment later they were joined, her long nails gouging his shoulders as she rode him, tears streaming down her cheeks, splashing onto Eli's chest, making him madder still. He thrust up into her, hard, no finesse, making her moan and hiss and cry out.

Then he lifted her up and off, making her moan again— from distress, most likely—only to flip her onto her back and plunge into her…and she clutched the wrinkled bedspread in her fists and arched into him, whimpering, her lower lip caught between her teeth a moment before she crossed her ankles at the small of his back and drove him higher, tighter, even though he knew he must be hurting her, if it'd been a year or more since she'd—

She sank her teeth into his neck, not hard enough to draw blood—he didn't think—but hard enough to make him jerk, then she licked the spot and blew on it, and he thought he'd lose his mind even as he did lose control, driving into her over and over and over until she screamed, clutching at his back as she tried to get on top of the orgasm.

But damned if he would let her, pushing her up, up, up until she had to curl forward to keep from banging into the headboard, shuddering his own release into her interminably pulsing warmth.

Afterward, annoyed, he collapsed on top of her, panting, fully expecting her to shove him off, get up, get dressed and demand he take her home. Instead she wrapped herself around him, all sweaty and smelling of woodsmoke and girly shampoo and sex, and whispered, her teeth grazing his earlobe, "How long until you're ready again?"

Floored, Eli pushed back enough to look at her. "You're not serious?"

"Oh, honey," she said, dragging her nails down his arms, making him shudder, making things stir he wouldn't've thought anywhere near ready to stir again, "I'm just getting started."

"Tess…you don't—"

Her fingers clamped around his arms, stopping him, her expression gone from postorgasmic mellow to oh-no-you-don't in two seconds flat. "Yes. I do." Her eyes glittered. "Burn this feeling out of me, Eli. Please."

Despite himself, his heart flipped over at the agony in those shiny eyes, at the soul-deep ache she had no idea how to ease. For some people—like his brother, like Tess—the end of a marriage was every bit as devastating as an actual death. But when he shifted to stroke his thumbs along her temples, she struck his hands away.

"No. I don't want you to make love to me."

His hands flat on either side of her head, Eli frowned at her. "You just want sex?"

"I just want sex."

"You just want me to make you feel good, is that right?'

"You got a problem with that?" she said, brows arched.

"Fine," he said, not sure why he was still pissed. "There any ground rules I should know about?"

Her pupils darkened. "None. I trust you."

"And why in the hell would you do that?"

"I don't know," she said, tearing up once more. Damn. An instant later, Mad Tess was back. "But just for a moment, you made me…forget." Her hands clamped around his face, she pushed against him, a tight smile pulling at her mouth when he responded. "Make me forget again."

Eli reached for another condom, thinking tonight was giving a whole 'nother dimension to that Good Samaritan thing.

\* \* \*

Nothing, Tess thought as she jerked awake the next morning, starts a girl's day out right like waking up to a Freddy Krueger scalp massage.

Swearing, she detached Maybelline—who hissed back— and bolted upright, immediately realizing that precipitous changes in altitude were to be avoided at all costs for the foreseeable future. And that she was naked in Eli Garrett's bed.

And nope, there was no "Did we…?" about this. Because they had. Oh, yes, indeedy, they had. Several times, in fact, before her anger was spent and many, many moons' worth of sexual frustration exorcised.

Groaning, Tess yanked the top blanket out from underneath the cat, stomped to the bathroom and did her thing, only to scream when she returned to the bedroom to find Eli standing there, dimples at a hundred percent, her sports bra dangling from one hand.

Growling, she snatched it out of his hand, scanning the room for the rest of her clothes. "That blanket sure looks better on you than it does on me," she heard behind her. As she irritably pondered how many times he'd undoubtedly used that line, he added, "Sleep well?"

She had, actually. Like the dead. "Guess I dozed off," she muttered, mincing past him to look on the other side of the bed.

"Honey, you passed out."

"I did not!" she said, twisting around, the velvety blanket's rasping across her nipples instantly hardening them. Or maybe that was Eli's knowing smirk.

"Like you would've voluntarily spent the night in my bed?"

Okay, there was that, she thought, clumsily dropping to her knees to look under the bed. Her head rebelled. As did her stomach. Especially when the damn cat decided to go after her bare toes. Yelping, Tess again jerked upright, catching her head in one palm before it rolled off her neck. Although the cat would probably love it. A new toy to bat around the room, yay.

Still cradling her head, she carefully hauled herself up to sit on the edge of the bed, wishing Eli would take pity on her and leave her to wallow in her mortification alone. But no.

Her stomach *boinged* when she felt the mattress shift. "Touch me and die."

And of course, that brought a warm, gentle palm to the top of her head. "Your head hurt?" Eli said softly, and many unkind thoughts leaped to her brain, mostly along the lines of how desperately she wanted Eli to not be kind. Or warm. Or gentle. Not now, at least. Last night had been another story. Last night had been—

"Oh, they haven't invented a word for how my head feels right now," she muttered. Just like there was no word for women who finagle their high school exes into pity sex. No, wait—actually, there were several. None of them flattering.

Her cell phone rang.

From her jacket pocket.

In, apparently, the living room.

She glared at Eli. Who kept on grinning. "Would you like me to get that for you?"

"If you wouldn't mind."

And during the approximately nine seconds he was gone, Tess found and put on the rest of her clothes, scattered willy-nilly about the room though they were. Eli returned and handed her the phone. And her jacket. Tess's heart nearly stopped when she saw Enrique's cell number.

"Everything okay?" she barked when he answered.

"Just what I was gonna ask you. Since you're not here."

Tess paused. "'Here' being…?"

"The house. Where the hell are you? When you didn't answer your phone I called your aunt. She's probably on her way over already."

Was there an award for Worst Morning After Ever? 'Cause Tess was at least a shoo-in for the finals. "You're supposed to have the kids until tonight—"

"Julia was up half the night, I think she missed you. So I figured I may as well bring 'em back since they were so miserable."

"They?"

"Okay, Micky, maybe not so much. But I'm not gonna drive up there and back twice in one day, am I?"

"For God's sake, Enrique—you only see them one weekend a month as it is—"

"Yeah, I know, I'm disappointed, too. So where are you?"

"At…a friend's. Since I *thought* I had the day to myself."

Turning, Tess caught Eli's frown. "I'll be home soon," she muttered, dialing Thea Griego's number when Eli stomped off.

*And it's a beautiful day in Bozoland,* she thought as Thea picked up, her "Tess? What's wrong?" delivered in the groggy voice of the mother of a one-year-old still not entirely down with the concept of sleeping through the night.

"Please tell me I didn't just wake you up."

"For you to do that, I'd've had to have been—" Thea yawned "—asleep." In the background, little Jonny happily squawked. "And you're calling when the sun's not even up yet, why?"

"Omigod, it isn't, is it?" Tess said, realizing that until that very moment, she hadn't thought her embarrassment level could spike any higher. She'd been wrong. "I have a huge favor to ask," she whispered. "First off, I need you to swear to anyone who might ask that I was at your place last night."

Silence. "Why? You kill somebody?"

"Worse," Tess muttered. "So will you?"

"Long as it doesn't involve the word 'accessory' in some way, sure, but—"

"And is there *any* way you could come pick me up and take me back home?"

More silence. "Um…pick you up from where?"

Somehow Tess doubted Thea'd buy her having spent the night by the side of the road. "Eli Garrett's."

"Lord, now I know I'm not awake yet. I could've sworn you said—"

"I did."

That got a far-too-gleeful cackle. "This just keeps gettin' better and better."

"Can you pick me up or not?"

"Do I have to put on makeup?"

"God, no."

"Then I'll be there in a few. Hang tight, honey."

Tess had no sooner shut her phone than she heard behind her, "I'm not good enough to take you home?"

She turned. And while Eli's insouciant smile and slouch against the door frame with his hands in his pockets might've said *Like I give a damn,* the sting of hurt in his eyes told another story entirely. What the hell?

"Oh, right," Tess said, dropping onto the edge of the embarrassingly rumpled bed to lace up her running shoes. "Like there'd be any way to explain to Enrique why *you* were bringing me home at the crack of dawn."

"He's there?"

"Brought the kids back early, yup." Slapping her hands on her thighs, she looked up. "Lucky me."

"Guess that makes two of us," he said, and Tess almost—almost—cringed at the bitterness spiking his words. "Because God knows I'm the last person you'd want to be associated with—"

"And don't even go there," Tess said, getting to her feet. "This isn't about you. It's about me not having the energy to deal with Ricky this early in the morning. It's also about me feeling like an idiot. Not because I slept with *you,* but because I…fell apart—"

He grinned. Not one of his best, but bright enough. "Several times, as I recall."

"Shut *up,*" Tess said, her face flaming, her nether regions tingling. Damn them. Fighting the urge to bury her face in her hands, she took a deep breath. "I used you, Eli. And I feel like crap about it."

His grin died. "And didn't I tell you this is exactly how you'd feel this morning? Although when you first came at me I sincerely doubted you'd be around for longer than twenty minutes—"

She grabbed a pillow off the bed and threw it at him. It went wide and scared the bejeebers out of the cat.

"It's not meant as a put-down, okay?" Eli said, swiping the pillow off the floor, tossing it back on the bed. "You were obviously upset. And a little drunk. I *knew* what you were asking for, even before you made it more than clear my hunch'd been dead-on. And if you noticed, I had no problem stepping up to the plate."

*Too true,* Tess thought as Eli came farther into the room, making her back up. A little. "Even so, I gave you plenty of opportunity to change your mind, to let me take you home before things got out of hand. Or maybe you don't remember—"

"I remember," she murmured, shutting her eyes.

"You know," Eli said after a moment, "maybe you wouldn't feel so bad if you'd just be honest about what happened last night. It was what it was. If I don't have a problem with that, why should you?" At the sound of Thea's old Jeep Cherokee pulling up in front of Eli's house, he nodded toward the window. "There's your ride," he said, snatching a hooded sweatshirt off the back of a chair and tossing it over. "It's cold. Put that on." Then he stomped off, boots pounding against the old wooden floor.

"Eli, I'm sorry—!"

Too late.

Soon as she heard stuff banging around in the kitchen, Tess scurried down the hall and through the front door, yanking on the hoodie as she practically flew into Thea's passenger seat. No fewer than three dogs of various sizes, shapes and lineages poked their heads through the gap between the bucket seats to offer greetings and/or condolences.

"Geez, mutts," the tiny blonde—wearing a down vest over wrinkled pink pajamas—said, shoving back assorted canine heads, "give the poor woman a break." She surveyed Tess for a few moments through a pair of perky round sunglasses before looking back out the windshield, her mouth twitching. "Rough night?"

Tess slumped down in her seat, snuggling farther into the warm, Eli-scented sweatshirt. Rats. "I seriously owe you for this."

"Think that's the other way around, cookie," Thea said as she backed out of Eli's drive. "Considering the backside-saving you did a couple months ago when everybody got the flu *except* the baby."

"Where is junior, anyway?"

"Back there somewhere, between the dogs." Startled, Tess twisted around to see the bundled up baby happily snoozing in his car seat. Thea cackled again. "Wow. This is just like high school, gettin' a girlfriend to cover your butt so your mother won't find out you went to some party you weren't supposed to."

"Yeah, well…I never did that."

*"Never?"*

"You weren't raised by a rabid Latina. My mother had spies everywhere." *Because that was a lot easier and less messy than personal interaction.* Gah, at this rate her brain would melt before breakfast. "I couldn't even look at a boy that my mother didn't hear about it before I got home."

"That sucks."

"Tell me about it."

Chuckling, Thea tucked a strand of barely combed, pale blond hair behind one ear as they pulled out onto the still-dark highway, the early-morning sun furtively peering through the pinons and live oaks choking the roadside. "So…what happened?"

Tess rolled her eyes in the blonde's direction.

"I got *that,*" Thea said, shrugging a dog head off her shoulder. "It's the how-in-the-hell? part I'm kinda vague on."

Shivering, Tess zipped the hoodie up higher. "So Ricky had the kids, right? Seizing my freedom, brief though it may have been, I went for a run, it started getting dark, Eli nearly ran me over with his truck, next thing I know I'm in his living room, stripping."

*"Sober?"*

"No."

"Ah." After a reflective moment, Thea glanced over. "I'm assuming there were bits between the almost getting run over and the stripping?"

"A lot less than you might think," Tess mumbled, then slumped down farther, palming her face. "I've never done anything even remotely like that in my entire life."

"Yeah, it must be hell, being perfect all the time."

Tess's eyes flashed to her friend. "What's that supposed to mean?"

"Honey, you know I love you—but sometimes it's like

you've set these impossible standards for yourself, like you're afraid anybody might find out you've got weak spots. So instead of occasionally releasing steam like any normal person, you let it all build up until you do something stupid."

"Like having meltdown sex with my old high school boyfriend."

"That would definitely qualify." Thea reached over, giving Tess's wrist a squeeze. "These things happen. No sense beating yourself up over it." She paused. "Although if you end up pregnant, that could be awkward."

Tess let out a dry laugh. "No worries there. My period's due in a couple of days. Which probably at least partly accounts for the meltdown. And we used condoms."

"Con*doms?*"

"Shut up."

"So," Thea said, clearly ignoring that last thing, "does this mean you and Eli, are, you know. An item?" Tess glared at her. She shrugged. "Had to ask."

"Would *you* recycle a high school boyfriend?"

"Good point. But maybe…"

"What?" Tess said, on guard.

"You could just…you know. Do the fling thing. Why not?" she said to Tess's snort. "He's hot, he's personable, he's obviously good with his hands…."

"You are so dead. And anyway, wasn't it just last year you were saying that Eli wasn't exactly the ripest apple on the tree?"

"True. But since he's now my stepdaughter's brother-in-law—"

Tess rolled her eyes.

"—I've gotten to know him some. Sure, he's still a goofball, but…" The blonde's eyes flashed to Tess. "He's not a kid anymore. There's a lot more beneath the surface than you might expect."

"Whether that's true or not, I'm not exactly keen on becoming another notch on Eli Garrett's bedpost."

"Hate to break it to you, honey," Thea said as she pulled into Tess's driveway. "But you just did."

And damned if she hadn't helped Eli do the carving, Tess thought on a sigh as she got out of the car, giving Thea a dejected little finger wave before she drove off.

"Mama!" Miguel dashed out the front door, throwing his small self into her arms like he hadn't just seen her the day before. About to drown in her own self-reproach, Tess yanked him close, breathing in that sweet-musky scent of little boy, thinking *Never, never, never, never again* as curly-topped Julia—not to be left out—carefully clung to the porch railing as she navigated the stairs. Singing "Jingle Bells." Sort of.

"Told you they missed you," Enrique said from the doorway to the stucco-and-brick facade house, his hands bunched in the pockets of his Arizona Diamondbacks baseball jacket. For an instant a trick of the light made him look like the man she'd once loved with all her heart, only to torque back into the bastard who'd shredded that heart into a million pieces. A moment later her Aunt Florita—frowning, arms crossed—appeared behind Enrique in spiked boots and tight everything else, despite her lack of boobage and surfeit of years.

"I'm so sorry," Tess said, to anybody and everybody, her arms full of her children, her heart of remorse. She kissed both kids, then rose, grabbing little hands before starting up the flagstone walk. "Obviously if I'd known," she said to Ricky, "I would have made other…arrangements."

"Don't worry about it," he said, then frowned. "Nice sweatshirt."

"Picked it up at a yard sale," she lied, ignoring her aunt's raised eyebrow. "I know it's way too big, but it's cozy as all get out—"

"You cut your hair?"

"Yeah," she said, thinking, *Geez,* now *nothing gets past you?*

He stared at her head for another couple seconds, then dug out his car keys. "One thing about hair, it always grows back, right? Hey, *cabritos,*" he called to the kids, squatting, "come give Daddy a kiss."

Honestly, Tess thought, it was like a wire had worked loose in her ex-husband's brain over the years. Sometimes the connections worked, and sometimes they didn't. Mostly, though, they didn't. And apparently hadn't for a long time.

His children duly kissed and hugged, Ricky stood, gave her what passed for an apologetic look, then started out to his truck, only to turn when he got there. "Oh, I forgot—I can't take the kids for Thanksgiving. I got…a conflict. That a problem?"

Tess crossed her arms. "For me? No."

Ricky looked at his son. "You don't mind spending the holiday with your mom, right?" Miguel shot Tess puzzled eyes, then shook his head. "See?" her ex said with what a poor imitation of his "old" smile. "So, Micky—you be good, okay? And I'll call you—"

"Tonight?"

"Not tonight, maybe tomorrow. Soon, okay?"

The boy hugged his father's thighs; to his credit, Ricky gave him another kiss before getting in his car and driving off. Flo wrapped her arm around Tess's waist, muttering, *"Pendejo,"* under her breath. And Tess highly doubted Flo meant *dumbass,* the most PG definition of the word.

Then her aunt's eyes dropped. The bandage had fallen off at some point during the evening's activities; although Tess had cleaned the scrape up, she hadn't bothered to redress it. *"Dios mio*—what happened to your leg?"

"I tripped over something while I was running," Tess said slowly making her way up the stairs with an I-can-do-it-myself toddler beside her. At the top, though, avoiding her aunt's X-ray eyes, she swung Julia up to pepper her soft little neck with kisses, making her giggle. "No biggie."

Once inside, she set her daughter down on the still-newish sculpted carpet she'd had installed before Enrique's last leave, a warm beige that was perfect with the light tan sectional she'd bought at the same time, its built-in recliner positioned so he could watch football on the flat-screen TV she'd gotten him for Christmas.

Nobody could say she hadn't tried. Nobody.

"Have the kids had breakfast yet?" she asked softly as old memories blurred uncomfortably into newer ones, a set of deep brown eyes morphing to hot, dark gold ones, welded to hers—

"Knowing Ricky? Probably not. How about you?"

"Um, no, I'm good for now," Tess said, backing away from her aunt's narrowed gaze, if not from the memories. "I had coffee and toast at Thea's. You know how early they eat on the ranch—"

"You know, you don't sound so good. Like maybe you're coming down with something?"

"Nothing a hot shower won't fix."

"Sure, then," Flo said, suspicion dripping from every word. "Take your time. I'll feed the kids."

Tess closed her bedroom door, thinking, *You're home now, everything's back to normal, just put last night's craziness out of your pretty little head....*

And there were Eli's eyes again, holding hers captive as he did things to her, for her, that, truth be told, Enrique had never even thought to.

Giving her head a hard shake, Tess twisted on the shower in the remodeled bathroom Ricky had hated on sight, saying it looked like somebody else's house, never mind that they hadn't lived here long enough that he should have thought anything one way or the other—

Moaning, Tess sank onto the whirlpool tub's tiled edge. Because, in the cold light of day, she had to admit…she hadn't been *that* drunk. Oh, she sincerely doubted she would have jumped Eli's bones sober—as in, no way in hell—but she hadn't exactly spaced what'd gone down after the bone-jumping part.

Or how many times.

Or how much, each time, she thought as she caught her haggard expression in the rapidly fogging mirror over the double vanity, a little more of the deadness around her heart she'd mistaken for stoicism had sloughed off, leaving in its place something tender and new and raw and frighteningly vulnerable. She really wasn't upset with herself simply because she'd had sex with Eli. It was what having sex with Eli had done to her that had left her shaking. And shaken.

Tess stood and stripped, daring to trace with a trembling hand the still-reddened patches left by Eli's late-day stubble across her belly and thighs and breasts. Who was this person who'd ceded so much control to another human being? Who'd known, at the time, exactly what she was doing? And who the hell was the man she'd *allowed* such power over her?

Worse, though, she thought as she jerked her gaze away from her reflection and stepped into the pounding shower, was that, mixed in with the regret…

Was the really scary feeling it could happen again.

## Chapter Three

No less pissed than he'd been an hour before, Eli stormed through the shop's door, the whining of table saws and pounding of hammers piercing his sleep-deprived brain. Yeah, Tess could play the "it's not you, it's me" card all she wanted, but she couldn't wait to get out of Eli's house, could she? To put her "mistake" behind her. True, maybe nobody could make you feel like dirt unless you let them—and maybe, considering their past, Tess wasn't totally out of line feeling the way she did—but that's exactly what he felt like. Dirt. Worse than dirt, like something disgusting on the bottom of somebody's boot.

But what Eli couldn't for the life of him figure out was why Tess's reaction was getting to him so bad. Wasn't like he expected anything more. Or less. And for sure it wasn't the first time he'd had a go-with-the-flow moment, even if the last one had been a while ago. Still. For somebody who'd been singing the no-strings song for a whole lot of years now, the last thing he'd expected was to…

Was to feel something for somebody he had no business feeling anything for. Not after all this time. Not after what he'd done. Not after one freaking *night,* for God's sake. What those feelings were, he couldn't even begin to sort out. But being with Tess…it just wasn't what he'd expected, that's all.

Just like getting his nose whacked out of joint wasn't what he'd expected, either.

"And what got up your butt?" his father launched at him as Eli strode across the dusty floor to the "kitchen"—a microwave, hot plate and coffeemaker set up on an old card table.

"Nothin'," Eli muttered, grabbing the coffeepot and sloshing some into his mug. "Just didn't sleep good last night."

At least it wasn't a lie. Especially after Tess passed out, and, instead of crashing, too, Eli found himself watching her sleep, hardly able to breathe through the "What the hell was that?" shock. Now, though, Eli didn't have to look at his father to see the what-now? squint. A squint not without cause. Not after some of the boneheaded stunts he and his brothers had pulled over the years. How his parents had survived raising four boys was nothing short of a miracle.

"You got troubles, son?"

Forcing a smile to his lips, Eli looked back at the old man. Jowly, balding and paunchier than was probably good for him, Gene Garrett may not have been as physically commanding as he'd once been, but that steely-blue gaze still lasered right through a person, even behind his glasses. His boys might not always agree with him, but not for a second would any of them think of disrespecting him.

"Nothing that's gonna cause the world to stop spinnin'," Eli said, clapping his father's shoulder before heading back to his own area of the shop, where a massive, carved headboard awaited staining. His father followed him, his arms crossed high on his chest. Eli glanced over.

"I'm okay, Pop. Really."

"No, it's not that." His father's gaze veered to the bed. "Guy called this morning and canceled."

"*What?* He can't do that, this is custom—"

"I explained all that, and he said he knows it means forfeiting the deposit and all, but…he said he was real sorry, but this just isn't a real good time to be spending big bucks on a headboard."

On a rough sigh, Eli dropped onto a nearby stool. "It hasn't been a *good time* for a while now. I mean, what the hell?" He scrubbed a hand along his jaw and let out another sigh as he glowered at the almost-finished piece. "It's not like I can just toss it in the back of my truck and go hawk it out on the highway, like Thea Griego does with those awful painted coyotes of hers. And don't you dare start up about how if I was led to make this thing, then it's gotta find a home."

"Patience has her perfect work, son," his father said, then smiled. "And God knows your mother and I have had ample opportunity to prove that particular passage over the years."

Sighing, Eli wagged his head, then got up and snatched a manila folder off the battered desk in the corner of the room. "You see this? It's my order folder."

"Looks a mite on the thin side."

Eli opened it and turned it upside down. A single sheet of paper fluttered to the gouged, sawdust-smeared floor.

"That was the bed, I take it?" his father said.

"Yep."

"Then there's somethin' else better waitin' in the wings, you'll see." Before Eli could groan, Gene added, "But we're doin' okay—you know what they say, when folks aren't buying new homes, they remodel. So we can always use you over on this side of the shop."

Eli glared at his father's back as he walked away. Yesterday, he'd been happy as a damn clam. Now the clam had just been shipped off to hell in a handbasket…a trip Eli'd taken a time or two before in his life.

Except now he realized it was up to him, whether it was a one-way trip or not. He could sit here and stew, or he could act like a grown-up and actually do something about it. Or at least try. Not about the canceled order, maybe—at least, not now—but about Tess? Yeah.

"Anybody got a phone book?" he yelled to the world at large. Seconds later one flapped to his feet, sending up a cloud of wood dust. With a nod to Jose, one of their employees, Eli snatched it up, elbowing off the cobwebs. Two years out of date but good enough. He flipped open the thin book, found Tess's number, then dug his cell phone out of his shirt pocket before he lost his nerve.

Maybe last night was a one-time thing—and maybe that's all it should ever be—but that didn't mean he and Tess Montoya didn't have a few things to clear up between them.

Like, now.

Toweling her hair, Tess stared at the ringing landline as though she'd forgotten it was there, since nobody called her on anything but her cell anymore, prompting her to wonder why she even kept the darn thing—

"You gonna get that or what?" her aunt yelled from down the hall.

"No," Tess yelled back.

Seconds later, Flo appeared at her door, phone in hand and speculative look on face. "It's Eli Garrett," she said, conveying a wealth of questions in three words. Because not only would Flo undoubtedly remember Tess's Eli phase, she would know Tess's and Eli's dealings since then had been virtually nonexistent.

Still, Tess played it as cool as a woman in a towel with recently applied beard burn across much of her person could. "Now what on earth do you suppose he wants? We haven't even spoken in years."

"I'm sure I have no idea," Flo said, handing over the phone. With a pointed look at Tess's abraded neck.

"Hot shower," she whispered.

"Whatever," Flo said, leaving the room and shutting the door behind her.

"Are you *insane?*" Tess said into the phone. "Why on earth—"

"Just making sure you're okay."

"Why wouldn't I be?"

"And maybe that's not an opening you want to be giving people, just at the moment. But that's neither here nor there. We need to get together. To talk."

"Eli… Last night… Nothing's—"

"Gonna happen. I know that. But there's stuff I need to get off my chest."

She tensed. "Then just say it."

"Dammit, Tess—where's it written you get to call all the shots? You don't have to accept my apology—"

"For what?" she said, thinking, *All the shots? How about any of the shots?* "Last night?"

"Hell, no, not for last night. Got no regrets about that. Never will. No, for what I did a dozen years ago."

Her chest cramped. "Eli—"

"I'm not offering up any excuses. But I'm truly sorry, Tess, for hurting you. I was then, even if I couldn't get over myself enough to say it. As for the other stuff…well. I'm not gonna

make any excuses for that, either. But I want you to know…
I'm not that person anymore."

"Why would I believe that?"

"I don't know," he said, sounding…tired. Sounding much too much like a man looking for comfort…making her much too much aware how willing she'd be to give it. Maybe. Under other circumstances. Like if they were two different people who didn't have some really bad history between them. "I don't suppose I've exactly given you—or anybody else—cause to believe I've changed," he was saying. "But last night…I guess it shook loose some stuff in my head I didn't even know was there. Ah, hell, I'm not even sure what I'm saying."

"Then don't," she said, fervently wishing he'd stop. Now. While she still had a grip on her anger. On her control.

"No, I've got to get this out." He paused, then said, "It's just…being with you again reminded me of what we had, I guess. What I threw away. But it's not like I was having some kind of let's-go-back-to-high-school fantasy or anything, okay?" Another pause. "Can I be honest?"

"I thought you were."

"Okay, more honest." He blew out a breath, then said, "Look, there's been a few women in my life—"

"A few?"

"Yeah, well, there were a lot of nonstarters in there. Even so—and I know this isn't gonna win me any points—most of 'em were…diversions. I'm not proud of that, but I never led any of 'em on, either. Given 'em any reason to think I was offering anything more than I was. I might've been a jerk, but I've always been an up-front jerk. But here's the thing, and I know this is gonna sound like a line, and a lame one at that…but it was different with you—"

"Oh, Eli, for God's sake—"

"I swear, Tess," he said, forcefully enough to shut her up.

She could count on one hand how often that'd happened. "You weren't a diversion, you were a helluva lot more than that. And I'm not sayin' that to get you back into my bed, or my life or anything. I know you weren't looking for anything last night except what happened, and that you're not likely to be looking for anything in the near future. Least of all from me. And that's okay, because I'm not, either. But I just couldn't stand the thought of you goin' for another second thinking…I don't know. That I didn't respect you or something. So. We clear on that?"

Another shudder of something damn close to terror snaked down Tess's spine. She had absolutely no idea how to respond, not to this…this take-charge person who in no way, shape or form resembled the laid-back, goofy Eli she remembered.

"Yeah, Eli," she said, startled to realize her voice wasn't steady. "We're clear."

As mud.

"Good. Then I'll let you get back to it. You have a good one."

Still wrapped in her towel, Tess sat on the edge of her bed for a long time after Eli hung up, feeling a little like she'd just seen a spaceship land outside her window—a combination of disbelief, apprehension and curiosity, all underpinned with the sneaking suspicion that life as she'd known it would never be the same.

Although there was no earthly reason for her to feel that way. Even if Eli had somehow done a one-eighty, what difference did it make? Like he said, she wasn't even remotely interested in starting up something. With anybody. *Because hope don't live here anymore,* she thought, tossing the phone onto the bed.

She dressed on autopilot, pulling items out of drawers and closets without thinking. Or, apparently, looking. Not until she returned to the kitchen, and her aunt's eyebrows shot up, did it hit her she was wearing her fave suede skirt, the designer boots she'd scored on eBay, a dressy sweater.

In other words, she'd dressed for work.

On Saturday.

*It's official, cookie,* she thought, dropping onto a kitchen chair—*you're losing it.* Or already had. Not that she'd never worked on Saturday, if that's the only time a client could look at houses, but when was the last time that had happened?

At the sound of the chair opposite dragging across the tiled floor, she peered over at Flo, whose heavy-handed makeup was not holding up well in the daylight. Something about the glittery eyeshadow.

"Okay," Flo said, "I was gonna keep my mouth shut—don' you roll your eyes at me, young lady—but firs' you get a call from Eli Garrett, an' now you come out here dressed like Miss Hot Shot Real Estate Lady when you haven't been to work in a month—"

"The two are not related." She didn't think.

"Maybe not. But somethin' is going on with you. An' I'm not leaving this house until I find out what. You can start by telling me where you really were las' night."

Tess looked around. "Where're the kids?"

"Out back, playing. Micky's keeping an eye on the baby. An' don' change the subject."

"Hard to do when I don't even know what the subject is."

Leaning back, Flo crossed her arms across her breasts, such as they were. "I got one word for you…*Eli?*"

"What makes you think—?" Her aunt laughed. "Glad you think this is funny." Suddenly starving, Tess got up to pour herself a cup of coffee before wrenching open a large metal tin on the counter filled with Little Debbie treats. She tried to remember how long ago she'd bought the chocolate-coated donuts. Couldn't. From outside, she heard Julia's belly laugh;

ripping the cellophane off the donuts, she walked to the window over the sink, then twitched back the curtain. Her babies were playing tag, an obviously still bummed Miguel letting Julia tackle him to the ground.

An entire stale, tasteless donut stuffed in her mouth, Tess's eyes smarted as she decided she was oddly grateful that the kids were as young as they were, that maybe their parents' divorce wouldn't scar them for life. But you know, considering the long stretches when they didn't see Enrique before, how much could his absence—his deliberate uninvolvement—affect them now?

Guilt, justifier of all things.

Three of the four donuts devoured, she grabbed her coffee and returned to the table, realigning the crooked salt and pepper shakers before cramming in the last doughnut. "Do I act like I think I'm perfect?" she asked with a full mouth.

"Where did that come from?"

"Something Thea said."

Underneath a head of stiff, black curls, Flo's brow crinkled. "I don' know about perfect, but…when you were real little, you'd go outside and play, bring half the dirt back inside with you. Pull out all your toys an' leave them all over creation. You know, like a normal kid?" Her mouth thinned. "Then your father walked out, an' everything changed. Suddenly, you couldn't stand messes. Wouldn't let yourself get dirty, never left a toy out of place. Your mother told me how you'd come home from school an' go straight to your room to make sure everything was exactly the way you left it. How you'd jump up from the dinner table to be the first to clear the dishes."

"So I became more orderly. What's wrong with that?"

Her aunt shrugged. "Nothing. On the surface. Only it was like after your father left, a switch flipped inside your brain, you know? An' suddenly it became all about control. About you having control over your universe. An' every time something threatened that control…" Her aunt shrugged again. "You got worse."

Tess stood to rinse out her coffee mug, setting it in exactly the same spot in the drainer she did every morning. Oh, God. But… Frowning, she looked at her aunt over her shoulder. "There was more to it, though, wasn't there? It was about me trying to please Mama."

Flo raised her coffee cup to her in salute.

Drying her hands on a dish towel, Tess returned to the table, sinking back into her chair with a sigh. "And after Ricky went into the service…all those months of feeling like my heart was in my throat…" Her eyes watered. "It was the only way I could keep from losing my mind."

"I know, *querida*," Flo said, leaning forward to briefly squeeze Tess's hand. Then she sat back again, her arms folded again. "Whatever happened las' night must've been really something."

Tess's eyes shot to her aunt's. "What makes you say that?"

"When was the last time we actually *talked?*" At Tess's blush, she added, "So. You spent the night with a man. An' now you're eaten up with guilt."

Tess's mouth flattened. "I'm not exactly proud of myself."

"One lapse don' make you a bad person, Tess." Her lip-sticked mouth quirked up. "An' not to put too fine a point on it…but if you ask me, you were way overdue." At Tess's slightly hysterical laugh, Flo added, "You're a young woman still. An' a divorce isn't a death sentence."

"It's only been a year—"

"You don' really expect me to believe that, do you?"

Tess bounced up out of her chair again and returned to the sink, her hand knotting atop the cold porcelain as she watched the kids through the window. It was true, she rarely talked

about her feelings, to her aunt or anybody. But after last night...
"Having a man around...it's just too confusing, trying to figure
out who I'm supposed to be. And anyway, then they leave, or
change their mind—or change, period—and then what?"

Flo came up to pull Tess close, as always the mother Tess's
own mother had never really been. "You know, baby doll, you
don' have to be strong all the time."

"What choice do I have?" she said, gesturing lamely toward the window, her babies. "It's not like their dad's exactly
picking up the slack."

"What about Eli?"

Tess frowned into her aunt's concerned eyes. "What
about him?"

"Does he like kids?"

"Oh, geez," Tess said on an airless laugh. "Eli as...as...
omigod, I can't even find the words. No, no, no..." Her hands
lifted, she walked back to the coffeemaker and poured herself
another cup. "*That* was an aberration, pure and simple. A
meltdown. And no how no way will it happen again."

"Why not?"

"You're not serious? Flo, you've heard the stories, same
as I have—"

"So maybe you shouldn't believe everything you hear."

The mug almost to her mouth, Tess lowered it, nonplussed.
This from the Gossip Queen of Tierra Rosa. "Yeah, well," Tess
said, "not only do I have firsthand experience—"

"Sixteen doesn't count."

"—but corroborative evidence abounds," she continued,
ignoring her aunt, "to back up my theory." Never mind his
parting words—that he had changed—gonging in her head.
"Eli and me...ain't gonna happen. End of discussion."

After a moment, her aunt returned to the table to retrieve
her own mug. "So. You going into work?"

"No," Tess sighed out. "Not sure I'm ready yet. Besides, it *is* Saturday."

"So?" Flo said, clicking back to the sink to rinse it out. "Give your brain something to do besides chew the past to bits. Find an outlet for all that excess energy. Not unless you wanna have another one of those *meltdowns*."

"I won't—"

"I'm off until Monday, I'll watch the kids since I know Carmen doesn't sit for you on the weekends—"

"I'm not going into work today! It was a mistake, okay?"

"Tell that to the boots and skirt," her aunt said, nodding at Tess's outfit, and Tess thought, *Rotten subconscious.*

"I know you needed some downtime after…after you signed the papers," Flo said gently. "But you gotta be goin' nuts by now, not working. So go into the office for a couple hours. Jus' to take your mind off…everything."

She could fight her, she supposed. Say, *No, don't wanna, not ready yet.* Except…Flo was right, damn her meddling little heart. A couple hours focused on the miserable real estate market would definitely take her mind off Eli, yep.

"You sure Winnie and Aidan don't need you?"

"I'm the housekeeper, not their slave. An' he's busy workin' on one of those big paintings for that show in New York, anyway. He won't even miss me. So *go.*"

So Tess hugged her aunt, grabbed a leather jacket from the coat closet and her purse from the counter, kissed her children—who'd tumbled back into the house, panting and looking for juice—bye-bye and told them she'd see them in a little while, to be good for Auntie Flo. Julia just waved and resumed her juice quest—little twerp—but Miguel gave her a look of such longing it nearly ripped her heart out.

"I'll be back soon," she said, leaning over to cup his cheek. "We'll make cookies, okay?"

"'Kay," he said, smiling a little.

And that, Tess mused as she eased herself behind the wheel of her slightly dented and dinged white SUV, just cried out for a serious caffeine and sugar injection, one Flo's wussy coffee and a pack of stale Little Debbies couldn't even begin to address.

Fortunately, Tess knew just where to get her fix.

## Chapter Four

She jerked the SUV into Ortega's tiny parking lot, realizing it'd been months since she and her girlfriends—Thea, her stepdaughter Rachel and relative newcomer Winnie Black, married to Flo's landscape-artist employer—had gotten together for their Wednesday afternoon gabfests, scarfing down churros and nachos or whatever Evangelista had left over after the lunch rush. After Tess's divorce, they'd tried to hold it together, but a bumper crop of new babies put paid to that idea. Not until Tess set foot inside the chile-, grease- and coffee-scented restaurant, though, did she realize how much her sanity had depended on those get-togethers. Maybe if they'd kept them going, last night wouldn't've happened—

"What can I get for ya?"

Tess smiled for the pimply, painfully young waitress who'd taken over for Thea, who'd realized a night-owl newborn and waitressing were not a good mix.

"Coffee. To go."

"Large or small?"

"Huge. Cream, no sugar. You're new?"

Pouring coffee into a foam soup container, the girl flashed a smile. "Just started last week. Name's Christine." She popped a plastic top on the cup, then wiped her hands on her jeans. "That'll be a buck-fifty."

"Actually, why don't you toss in one of those cinnamon rolls, too?"

"You know, those've been sittin' out since this morning. We've got a fresh batch just about to come out of the oven if you don't mind waiting."

"You, honey, are an angel," Tess said, right about the same time she heard, "How's the leg?" right behind her. Yeah, just who she wanted to run into. Especially as, awake and sober, the tingling stuff from the night before?

Ten times worse.

"Leg's fine," she said, turning back to the counter, thinking if she concentrated *real* hard Eli wouldn't be there when she looked around again.

"Workin' today?"

So much for that. "Maybe."

Sliding up on the stool right next to her, Eli chuckled, all low and deep and rumbly. That, too, was ten times worse, awake and sober. You would think messing around six ways to Sunday would have gotten it out of her system.

But no.

"Us, too," Eli said. "Dad's got a big job installing next week, so couldn't take the day off."

"Oh. That's good, then," she said, facing him. Acting like she had spontaneous, combustible sex with the random ex-boyfriends all the time. "That you're so busy."

"Yeah. It is," he said, facing away. "Hey, Chrissy," he called out to the waitress, his voice just as warm and sunshiny as it could be. "Gimme a half dozen breakfast burritos, okay?"

"Got it!"

"That cold all gone?"

The girl beamed. "Sure is. I did just like you said and drank a ton of hot tea, and it hardly even bothered me at all."

"Told you. What?" he said to Tess, who swung her head back around.

"Nothing," she muttered, and Eli swiveled his stool, plunked his elbows on the counter and resumed his conversation with Christine, now serving a couple at one of the tables.

"How's your grandmother getting on?"

"Oh, she's fine now. She'd just forgotten to eat breakfast and fainted, was all. That reminds me—she said to thank you for cleaning out her gutters last week."

"No problem," he said with a bright, completely nonflirtatious smile, then swung back around, pinning Tess with his gaze. *"What?"*

"Who *are* you?"

He laughed, then tilted his head. "I like that sweater on you."

"Um, thanks?"

"Although…"

"Don't even go there," she muttered because she knew exactly where he was going. As did her nipples, which perked up quite nicely at the unspoken innuendo.

"You know, you really need to loosen up some."

"Yeah, like it worked so well the first time."

"And the second. And the third—"

"Oh, for heaven's sake—" Her head whipped around. "Is this the way it's gonna be from now on?" she whispered. Savagely. "You never letting me forget my one…indi-discretion?"

Last thing she'd expected was for her voice to go rogue on her. Or for a pair of contrite golden eyes to find hers. Which didn't at all jibe with the soft, intense, "Maybe I don't want you to forget it," that followed.

Christine picked that moment to return with Tess's bagged cinnamon roll, bless her soul. Armed with her coffee and snack, Tess turned smartly on her skinny boot heel…and ran smack into some dude who'd come up behind her.

"Oh! Sorry!" she said to the cowboy as the flimsy lid flew off the coffee, which erupted all over her jacket. She yelped, wondering when she'd turned into such a klutz, as Eli grabbed her from behind to keep her from creaming the poor guy.

"You okay?" Eli asked, so gently tears crowded her eyes, which was even more ridiculous than the tingling and all that it represented. "Honey," he said to the startled waitress, "you mind bringing us a damp cloth or something?"

But before she could scurry off, Evangelista Ortega herself appeared, three hundred pounds of take-no-crap efficiency. "Gimme your jacket," she demanded, practically ripping it off Tess as she barked to the new girl to get another cup of coffee, for God's sake, what was she waiting for?

Diplomacy had never been Evangelista's thing.

Her gigantic bosoms shimmying magnificently, she carefully blotted up the coffee from the leather, blew on it until she was satisfied and handed the coat back to Tess.

"There. Good as new. But I never see you this jumpy before." Her black gaze zeroed in on Eli. "*Dios mio*—don' tell me *you're* back in the picture?"

"No!" Tess said, her face flaming. "Just a coincidence, us running into each other…" She cleared her throat, which also apparently sparked An Idea. "Hey, Eva, you don't by any chance know of anybody looking to sell their house who might need a listing agent?"

Black brows lifted. "Why you asking me?"

"Because nothing gets past you?"

Her mouth pulled down in a this-is-true expression, Eva nodded. Then sighed. "Other than that old junker up on Coyote Trail? *Nada*."

"Charley Harris's place, you mean?" Eli put in. Because he was clearly harder to get rid of than mold.

"That's the one. His kids've been trying to unload it for more'n a year now."

"Yeah, I know that place," Tess said. "My partner had it listed for a while."

"My cousin, she did some cleaning for the old guy who used to live there," Evangelista said, clearly unconcerned about her other customers. "Said the inside looks like something out of a vampire movie. Guy was a real pack rat, she said, although they probably got rid of all the crap by now, if they've been trying to sell it. But the kitchen and bathrooms?" She rolled her eyes. "God himself couldn't move that place. Oh, here's your food," she said to Eli, peering through her glasses at the ticket. "Put it on your tab?"

"Yeah," he said, hefting the plastic bag as he slid off the stool. With a nod to Tess, he started toward the door.

"By the way," Evangelista called, "how were those enchiladas? I tried something a little different with the sauce, did you notice?"

Shouldering the door open, Eli turned, dimples flashin'. "Can't say as I did."

"They weren't too hot, then?"

His eyes touched Tess's. "Nope, not too hot at all," he said, then pushed his way outside.

"Man," Evangelista said on a wistful sigh as they both watched Eli through the plate glass window as he got into his truck, "if I was twenty years younger, I would be all *over* that *hombre*."

Blowing out a breath, Tess gathered up her replaced cup

of coffee and the battered roll in its bag, refusing to meet Evangelista's questioning gaze before hotfooting it out herself. She'd intended to head straight for the little office on Main Street she'd shared with Suzanne Jenkins, her partner; instead she headed east, toward the house in question. Normally she'd never go after one of Suz's old listings—the real estate equivalent of dating your best friend's ex—but times being what they were, she'd take what she could get.

As far as listings went, that is.

She pulled up in front of the secluded old adobe and got out, getting a scolding from a crow atop a nearby telephone pole, a thick layer of pine needles cushioning her footsteps as she walked up the flagstone path. From the outside, the pinon-smothered house didn't look too bad—the adobe was solid, the pitched, tin roof seemed in fairly decent condition. On the small side, maybe, but not everybody needed or wanted a big house. And—she turned—the setting was spectacular, with great, sweeping views of sky and mountains and valley.

*Location, location, location…*

Shivering in the frigid breeze, Tess tiptoed around the house's perimeter, peering inside cloudy windows, the turquoise-painted wooden trim peeling and pockmarked with dry rot…an easy-enough fix. Heck, once the trim was replaced, she could paint it herself if she had to. The inside, though…oh, dear. Even through the murky glass, she could see the outdated kitchen cabinets and countertops, the scarred, smoke-smudged walls, the worn shag carpeting in the living room.

She got back in her car, giving the poor, neglected house a final glance. Were these people off their nut? Who on earth put a house on the market in that condition? Especially these days?

Was she off *her* nut, even considering taking the thing on? Twenty minutes later, she walked into the office, nearly giving Candy Stevens, their receptionist, heart failure. "What in the blue blazes are you doing here?" the well-past-forty redhead barked from behind her desk by the front door.

"Got a divine message I was supposed to come back today," Tess said, crossing to her side of the one-room office. Dust of postapocalyptic proportions lay thick on her desk.

"You might've given us some warning," Candy—whose fashion philosophy pretty much began and ended with push-up bras, fringe and Aqua Net—said, following. Today's ensemble included a snuggly sweater, tight jeans and cowboy boots never meant to come anywhere near a horse. "I haven't even dusted or anything over here in weeks."

"So I noticed." Tess set her coffee and roll on top of her printer, then shrugged out of her jacket, hanging it on the back of her chair. "Where's Suze?"

Who, knowing her partner, would be less than thrilled by her return. Suze wasn't real big on sharing. Except for rent and utilities.

"On vacation," Candy said, madly taking a feather duster to shelves and things, stirring up a lot more dust than she was dispatching. "She'll be back Monday. Oh, my goodness, honey—you got a rash or something on your neck? You're all red—"

"It's nothing!" Tess said, only to be suddenly squished against Candy's copious bazooms.

"God, I missed you," the older woman whispered, as though somebody might be eavesdropping. Then she let Tess go. "You know I love Suze to death, but she's…"

"Suze," Tess said, smiling. Heaven knew why Suze had taken Tess under her wing, mentoring Tess into as good an agent as she was. Or at least had been. But the four-times-married blonde's piranha-esque tactics were legendary.

Woman could probably sell property to the dead. So why hadn't she been able to unload the house up on the hill?

"So I see she dropped the Coyote Trail listing?" Tess said, settling in front of her computer.

"More like the sellers dropped Suze," Candy said, butt twitching as she returned to her own desk by the front door. "Birdbrains. They wanna dump it but won't spend a dime on updates. Suze took a stab at selling it as a fixer-upper, but in this market? No way."

"So there's no lockbox?"

Candy's eyes snapped to hers. "You went up there?"

"Just a little bit ago, yeah. I think it has potential."

"For the Addams family, maybe."

Tess smiled. "You got the clients' contact info?"

Now Candy frowned. Carefully. "Well, sure, it's still in the system, but honey…you can't be serious."

"What can I say? I'm up for a challenge."

Anything to take her mind off Eli, she thought, catching herself moments before she touched the aforementioned "rash" on her neck. But not before the memory of how that rash got there started up the tingling. Again.

"There's challenges and then there's banging your head against a wall. Sugar, I hate to break it to you, but business hasn't exactly picked up while you were gone. In fact…" She sighed. "Suze said if things didn't improve by the end of the month she'd have to let me go. So I'm thinking this might not be the best time for you to be thinking about getting back in the groove."

A feeling like hot steam flashed up the back of Tess's neck. "Nobody's letting you go, Candy," she said, even as she wondered how she planned on making good on her promise. A moment later, she had the contact info on the screen in front of her; five minutes after that, she'd arranged to meet Fred and Gillian Harris at the house the following Monday.

She hung up the phone to see Candy wagging her head. "Honey, you are one serious glutton for punishment."

Yeah. Tell her about it.

Once inside the house on Monday morning, Tess decided it reminded her of a tired housewife who'd given up the good fight. Unfortunately, houses were not capable of dragging their saggy butts to the gym or touching up their own roots.

According to Fred and Gillian-please-call-me-Gilly, the late-middle-aged, well-heeled sibling duo currently dogging Tess's heels on her preliminary walk-through, their father had succumbed to Alzheimer's more than a year before, necessitating their putting him in a care facility. Clearly the poor guy hadn't been able to keep the place up for some years before that. Still, there was a lot of charm left in the old girl, if you knew what to look for.

How to bring her back to life.

But it hadn't taken Tess five minutes to size up the pair as the "just make it happen" type. These days, though, *making it happen* took a bit more effort than simply sticking a For Sale sign out by the road and slapping the place up on the Internet.

"It's already been on the market more'n a year," Fred said to Tess's back as she frowned at the worn, fake brick flooring, the dark, depressing cabinets. Big difference between retro and regressive.

"So I heard," Tess said with a slight smile as she peered inside the good-size pantry, recoiling at the telltale scent of rodent droppings.

"We really need to sell it," Gilly said. "For Dad." The neatly coiffed brunette glanced at her brother, then back at Tess. "The place we've got him in…it's good. And, well, pricey."

As were, Tess surmised, the gal's diamond earrings and Fred's watch. So she wasn't exactly getting an indigent vibe here, even if she didn't doubt Charley's new "home" was costing an arm and a leg. Still, she knew she had to tread very carefully if she wanted this listing. Which she did, so badly she could taste it. To feed her sense of self-worth almost more than her bank account. Not to mention help Candy keep her job.

"I suppose…" Fred exchanged another glance with his sister. "We could lower the asking price…"

"Actually, I think you should raise it. A lot." As expected, four eyes popped wide open. While Tess had them in stunned mode, she moved in for the kill. "Slow market or no, there's still some demand for these old adobes—"

"Then—"

"—as long as they're in tip-top condition," she said, and both faces fell. Gee, big surprise. "For the most part, people are looking for vacation homes," she continued, "someplace to spend weekends skiing or escape from the summer heat. Soon as they get the keys, they want to walk through the front door, kick off their shoes off and run a hot bath, not start gutting old kitchens. And cleaning up mouse droppings."

Gilly's eyes darted around the kitchen. "You think there's mice?"

"Oh, I'd stake my life on it. Look," Tess said, gently, but firmly, when they both made a face, "you gave the fixer-upper plan a year and it didn't work. Be honest—would *you* want to live here? In the shape it's in now?"

Another shared glance. Then the woman said, "What…do you suggest?"

Tapping her pen on her clipboard, Tess looked around, pretending to consider. "I'm not talking major remodel, but the kitchen and bathrooms need some serious updating. New cabinets and countertops, tile floors. And the shelves in the den? Really awful."

"Dad built those himself," Gilly said, sighing. "He was so proud." She looked at the seventies-era harvest gold stove. "And the appliances?"

"Wouldn't hurt to change them out. Don't have to be top of the line, but they should at least be from this century."

The siblings looked at each other, then back at Tess. "What kind of money are we talking?" Fred asked.

"Well…you could easily sink forty, fifty grand into the place—"

"Good God!"

"But twenty-five should cover it."

"Forget it—"

"Oh, come on, Freddy, it's not as if we don't have it. And if she can get us—" Gilly turned to Tess. "How much?"

Tess wrote a number on her pad, then turned it around to show them.

"Oh, my," Gilly said, hand on cheek.

Fred frowned. He seemed to do that a lot. "But there's no guarantee it'll sell."

"No, there's not," Tess said easily. "And I understand your concerns, I really do. But you know, we're so close to Taos and Santa Fe…once the house is fixed up, even if it doesn't sell it would make a terrific vacation rental. So there's another option. We could manage the property for you. You wouldn't have to do a thing." When the two exchanged another glance, Tess picked her purse up off the chipped Formica counter. "Tell you what…why don't I give you a few minutes to talk it over between you? I'll just wait outside."

Tess crossed to the kitchen patio door, the glass practically opaque from God-knew-how-many years' worth of grime and dust. French doors, both in here and the living room, would be spectacular…

Five minutes later, if that, she heard the door slide open behind her. "Ms. Montoya?"

Tess turned, trying not to look *too* eager. "Yes?"

"Tell you what," Fred said, hiking up his designer jeans as he walked out onto the redwood deck. "If you can bring in the renovations for twenty grand, we've got a deal. I'm not real keen on the vacation house idea, but Gilly seems to think it could work. And we like your style." He extended his hand. "So. You've got the listing. Until Christmas."

Tess's stomach dropped. "But…that's less than two months! Six is more customary."

"If you can't sell it before the holiday vacation season starts, we might as well rent it out."

That'll teach her to come up with brilliant ideas.

"And one more thing—long as you're hirin' a carpenter anyway…you know Gene Garrett?"

"Uh…sure…"

"He and I went to school together, I know he's got a cabinetry shop in town. If I gotta spend the cash to fix this place up, might as well toss some of it his way, you know what I mean? Especially these days, I imagine he could use the business. Betcha also if you mention my name? He'll give us a good deal."

Lord save her from cheapskates. And heaven knew there were other carpenters in the area she'd much rather hire, for obvious reasons. But if Gene Garrett was part of the deal, *she'd* deal.

"I'll get in touch with him this afternoon," Tess said, shaking Fred's hand.

"For crying out loud, dog," Eli yelled at Blue, his father's old Heeler, when the mutt started yapping up a storm at the front of the shop. "What's your problem?" A moment later, light flashed across the front room as the door swung open.

"Anybody here?" Tess called out.

Thinking, *What the hell?* Eli set down the sander and walked out front, his fingers jammed in his jeans' pockets. Busy with the dog, Tess didn't see him at first, giving him time to give her a nice, leisurely once-over. Tight jeans. High-heeled boots. A soft, body-hugging sweater too long for her leather jacket. Big old dangly earrings. An aura of purpose he still wasn't used to.

"Slumming?" he said mildly, making her jump. She straightened, clutching a purse bigger than she was to her side, out of which she dug his sweatshirt.

"Um...I brought this back," she said, handing it to him, then looking around. "Your dad here?"

"Nope. Out on that install. So's everybody else. Just me and the dog holdin' the fort. What can I do for you?"

Yeah, the double meaning had been sorta deliberate.

Not that she'd give him the satisfaction of reacting. Except for her eyes. Gal's eyes gave her away every time. And why he was goading her, he had no idea. Wasn't like he expected, or wanted, anything to come of it. Then again, maybe that was the point. That, knowing he was perfectly safe, he could goad all he wanted.

Safe from her anyway. Safe from himself? Maybe not so sure about that.

"I just got the Coyote Trail listing," Tess said, and he dragged his head back from wherever it had wandered.

"You're kidding."

"Why does everyone keep saying that?"

"Because the place is a dump?"

"It's not a dump, it just needs...a little TLC."

"Honey, what that place needs is ten years of intensive care."

"In an ideal world, maybe. But what I got the Harris spawn to agree to is the rehab equivalent of Botox. In any case, Fred

Harris apparently went to school with your dad, wants to give him the work—"

"Wait a minute…you actually talked them into fixing the place up?"

She almost smiled. "I can be very persuasive," she said, her voice all low and sexy, and Eli literally bit his tongue to keep from saying something stupid. Instead he squatted to scratch Blue's ears.

"Hate to be the bearer of bad news, but Dad's booked through January. Unless y'all can wait until February—"

"No, it has to be done immediately. I only have the listing until Christmas."

"That's insane."

"Tell me about it." For the first time, doubt wrinkled her forehead. "Are you sure he couldn't squeeze this in? Somehow?"

"You're talking, what? Kitchen and bath update?"

"And redoing some of the built-ins, and the window trim…"

"Then I think it's safe to say Dad's not gonna be able to 'fit you in'." To prove his point, he walked over to the old, beat-up desk on the other side of the room and picked up a bulging folder.

"Crap," she said. "Not that I'm not thrilled for your dad, having so much work."

"Of course, if you're really hard up…" Eli grinned. "There's always me."

"Um, I think I'll pass." But she didn't sound all that happy with her decision. Or him, hard to tell. "Were you always this…cocky and I somehow missed it?"

"I prefer to think of it as charming."

"As I said."

Eli crossed his arms. "How come you didn't call first, save yourself a trip?" *Saved yourself the awkwardness of having to talk to me.*

"I did. Nobody answered. Kept getting the machine."

"But I've been right here…" Eli glanced over at the phone, blinking its little butt off. *Messages, 3.* "How many times you call?"

"Three."

"Guess I couldn't hear over the sander."

"Guess not," Tess said, starting for the door.

"You'd rather lie naked on an anthill than work with me, wouldn't you?"

Slowly, she turned, her brows drawn. "Something like that, yeah."

"Funny, I would've never pegged you as somebody who'd judge a person without having all the facts."

The frown deepened. "Is that what you think I'm doing?"

"Frankly, yeah. Because apparently what I said, about how I've changed? Didn't even register. And excuse me, but it's just the tiniest bit annoying that you're assuming a lot based on what basically amounts to hearsay."

"You're saying…the gossip's untrue?"

He hesitated. "Not all of it, no. But…" Digging his fingers into the back of his neck, Eli tried to pull in enough breath to ease the tightness in his chest. "But what you hear…I'm more than that, Tess. I swear."

"Then if there's some salient fact I'm missing, by all means, clue me in."

A couple of beats passed before Eli walked over to an old futon on the other side of the room and sat on the arm. Unfortunately, this wasn't just any random piece of furniture, but the very one where they both lost their virginity many moons ago. When Tess sucked in a breath, Eli softly laughed. "Yep. It's still here. Even if the two kids who enjoyed each other on it aren't."

"Eli…don't—"

"You know, I still see glimpses of the crazy, funny girl who could light up a room just by walking into it. Not to mention the one who never had a bad word to say about anybody. It's not that I don't understand why she doesn't come around much anymore," he said quietly, "but I sure do miss her. Like I said, I know I hurt you back then. And I don't even expect you to accept my apology. But seems to me that girl wouldn't still be obsessing about a failed high school romance."

Tess gave him a long, penetrating look, then let out a sigh that seemed more perplexed than mad. "First off, that girl? I'm not all that sure she ever really existed. Secondly, I'm hardly obsessing about our breakup. What still bugs me, though, is that you never gave me an explanation. Not even when you called to apologize the other day. So, combined with your reputation? The anthill's looking pretty good."

Eli's brow knotted. "You never asked."

"I shouldn't have *had* to ask! Because I deserved an explanation. I deserved…" She pushed out a breath. "More. And I'd expected more from you. Hence the mop. And the anthill thing—"

"I was scared, Tess. That's it, bottom line. I was terrified out of my skull."

"Of what? Me? That's—"

"Hell, yeah, you. I had no idea it was possible to feel so strongly about somebody at, what were we? Seventeen? And I couldn't deal with it. So I snapped."

For a moment—barely—he thought he saw a glimmer of sympathy in her eyes. "For heaven's sake, Eli, it wasn't like I expected us to get married or anything."

"Logic didn't even enter into it," he said, getting to his feet. "All I knew was, things were happening way too fast, and I wasn't even remotely ready. And I had no earthly idea how to tell you that."

She glanced away, like she was trying to process this. But when she looked back, the sympathy had gone buh-bye. "And somehow this translated into going after Amy Higgins?"

Cripes, it was like having a conversation with two different people. He half expected to see her eyes glow red.

"It was sorta the other way around, truth be told. I swear," he said when she huffed out a sharp laugh. "But it never felt right. We broke up, like, a month later—"

"Yeah. I remember. I also seem to remember you recovered from her quickly enough, too. And the one that followed. And the one that followed after that—"

"Didn't take you long to hook up with Enrique, either, as I recall."

She flinched, and Eli finally got it, that this wasn't only about the two of them. That somebody else far more recently than him had hurt her, too—

"Actually, it was more than a year," she said in that wind-outta-her-sails voice.

And once more Eli happened to be in the line of fire, just like he'd been the other night.

"But from everything I heard," she said, "your pace sure didn't slow down any—"

"You were away for several years, don't forget."

"True. But when I returned…well, let's just say the broken heart trail didn't seem to be in danger of stopping anytime soon. Oh, come on, Eli," Tess said, revving up again, "you know you can't go anywhere in this town without running into somebody hot to tell you the latest, good or bad. And people have long memories, especially those well-meaning souls eager to assure me—even after all this time—I was better off without you, that the boy who skipped on me just kept on skipping, from one chick to another like rocks in a creek."

Her words pelted him like sleet, stinging all the more because they were truer than he wanted to admit, inflicting enough pain to make him say, "Wow—you must've been *really* out of it to end up in my bed."

Color flared in her cheeks. "Already established that," she muttered, this time making it all the way to the door, and Eli wondered if he'd ever learn to think before he spoke.

"It's okay, I completely understand," he called after her. "But if you get desperate, you know where to find me."

After one final, flummoxed glance, Tess walked out, slamming the door shut behind her.

Which Eli stared at for a lot longer than he should've probably, but the feeling-like-dirt feeling had come back with a vengeance, clobbering him upside the head over and over and over. Because no matter which way you looked at it, Tess was right. If not about all of it, about enough to completely justify her attitude. Because he had hurt her, he hadn't bothered to tell her why and he'd definitely provided plenty of fuel for the gossip mill these past several years. So from where he was sitting, he had some serious atoning to do. And some lame "I'm sorry, I'm not that man anymore" wasn't gonna cut it—somehow he had to *prove* to Tess he'd changed.

For his own peace of mind, if nothing else.

Mulling that over, Eli trudged back to work, letting himself get caught up in his tasks until, maybe two hours later, the phone rang.

And yeah, he might've smiled for a second when he saw the caller ID, relishing the victory. Except underneath the relishing, something else kinda hummed. Like the sound from those overhead wires they said messed with your brain or something.

"Garrett's—"

"Fine, so you win. I've called every carpenter within fifty miles, and there's nobody else available unless I want to bring in somebody from Albuquerque, and no way are the Harrises gonna fork over the extra cash for that. So when can you meet me at the house to give me an estimate?"

"You sure do cut to the chase, don't you?"

"The groveling stings less that way."

Eli chuckled. "In an hour good for you?"

"That's fine. Long as you don't mind the kids being with me."

The humming got louder. "Not at all," he said, looking out the wood-dust-coated window. Telling himself he was strong enough to avoid that particular pull. That if he wanted an opportunity to prove himself, this couldn't be a better one. He smiled. "Especially since you clearly need a chaperone. Or two."

"Bite me," she said and hung up.

## Chapter Five

An hour gave Tess just enough time to pick up her kids and put her pride back in the dungeon where it belonged. Umbrage was all well and good in its place, but it had *no* place in business. And business was what this was all about, she thought when Eli knocked on the house's open door, the dog bounding inside ahead of him.

And only what it was about.

"Cool!" Miguel said, immediately on his knees to hug the dog. "What's his name?"

"Micky! Be careful—!"

"It's okay, he loves kids," Eli said, then gave Micky a half smile. "And his name's Blue. I'm Eli."

One eye on the dog and Julia balanced on one hip, Tess literally met Eli halfway, in the middle of the musty, mud-colored carpeted living room. But before she could open her mouth, Eli said, "You really okay with this?"

"I'm…" A smile tugged at her mouth. "Getting there. In any case, I've had lots of practice making the best of a bad situation."

With a soft laugh, Eli headed for the kitchen, clipboard in hand. "Good to know. Because I'd hate to mess up the whole symbiotic thing we've got going on here."

"Symbiotic?"

"Yeah, you know, when each entity needs the other to survive?" At her poleaxed look, he grinned. "Mom was one of those word-a-day freaks. Her two goals, when we were kids, were making sure we knew the right way to hold a fork and force-feeding us a whole bunch of ten-dollar words. Because God forbid anybody take us for hicks," he said, carefully opening a kitchen cabinet door about to fall off its hinges, then brushing dust from his hands. "Yep, place looks about as bad as I remember."

From the living room, Tess could hear Miguel chattering to Blue. Hiking a squirmy Julia higher on her hip, she glanced through the doorway to see her son perched on the edge of the raised hearth, the dog sitting in front of him with his head cocked—

"You've been here before?" she said, Eli's words sinking in.

"Yep." Leaving the door ajar, Eli squatted to inspect one of the lower cupboards. "Used to come over now and again to check up on Charley after he started going downhill."

"Huh. Fred didn't mention that little detail."

"Not sure he knew about it, to be honest," Eli said, straightening to make notes on the clipboard. "Dad did, mostly, but I'd stop by once a week or so. Bring Charley a stuffed sopapilla from Ortega's. Or a beef and potato burrito. Man, he did love those. Grinned like nobody's business the minute I'd unwrap it—"

"Down!" Julia screeched. "Down, down, down!"

Realizing she and Eli would never be able to hear each

other if she didn't give in, Tess lowered the child to the dusty tile floor; immediately she zoomed off to join her big brother. Eli glanced over, his expression…odd.

"Sorry," Tess said. "What she lacks in vocabulary she makes up for in volume."

"And earnestness."

"That, too. My little toughie."

"Like her mother," he said, opening another door. "And that was a compliment, so don't go gettin' all bent out of shape."

She smirked. "Wouldn't dream of it." Wandering away to keep an eye on her little hooligans, their high voices echoing in the empty space, she shook her head. "I just wonder why Charley's kids didn't get him out of here sooner."

"You'd have to ask them that. Although I think you can guess." When she turned, Eli rubbed his thumb and fingers together. "As in, they didn't want to see their potential inheritance dwindle by spending it on their own father. Fortunately, he never got too bad—never wandered down Main Street naked or anything. And he always knew who Dad and I were. It was just… It was like he was in a dream. In his own little world."

"Still," Tess said, facing her kids again. "That's so sad. To think…" She shook her head.

"If it makes you feel better—" she heard Eli's metal tape measure rattle across the countertop "—I don't think he was unhappy. Or lonely. But I know what you mean. I can't imagine leaving my folks to the mercy of whoever happened to be available."

"I couldn't do that to Flo, either."

The tape measure snapped back. "Still on the outs with your mom, then?"

"She has her life, I have mine," Tess said softly, her heart swelling with love for those hooligans even as old hurts tried to wind themselves around it.

"She sees her grandkids, though, right?"

"Once in a blue moon, maybe. She's…not much of a kid person."

In the empty room, Julia let out one of her belly laughs, probably at something her brother did. Tess nearly jumped when Eli's hand landed on her shoulder—*bzzzt*—for an instant before he swept past her out of the room. "Okay, that's it for in here," he said as Tess told herself she didn't miss his touch. Really. "Let's go check out the bathroom. No telling how bad that must be by now—"

"I got Blue to sit, Eli!" Miguel said, accosting the poor man the instant he hit the living room, as he was wont to do with every male he met these days. Sensing the void, Tess supposed, left by his rarely-there father, their infrequent visits infected both with the boy's wary neediness and his father's discomfort or guilt or whatever. "Wanna see?" Miguel said, hopping about like a curly-headed little flea.

Eli halted, briefly, giving Miguel a strained smile. "Maybe later," he said, with an equally brief, strained glance at Julia, who'd taken up the flea dance, too, accompanying herself by "singing" at the top of her robust little lungs.

As Eli continued down the hall, Miguel frowned at Tess, not so much hurt as confused. *Make that two of us,* Tess thought. Seeing Eli with Christine in Ortega's, listening to him talk about how he and his dad kept tabs on poor old Charley…why would he be standoffish with her kids? Although…

"It's okay, baby," she said. "He's just busy. Um…watch Julia for a sec, okay?"

"'Kay."

Busy poking at tiles and such, Eli didn't at first notice Tess when she leaned against the bathroom door. "Sorry about the ambush," she ventured. "Micky tends to gravitate to Y chromosomes like metal filings to a magnet."

Eli flashed a glance in her direction. "No problem."

"Even so…all he did was ask you to watch him get your dog to sit."

Retracting his tape measure from across the grime-encrusted sink cabinet, Eli gave her a steadier look, his normally mischief-riddled eyes flat. "Just trying to keep things moving, that's all," he said mildly.

"You don't like kids?"

Eli's brows shot up, followed by a startled laugh. "Just because I didn't stop and watch Miguel and the dog, you automatically assume I've got a problem with kids?"

"You looked…pained, is the only word I can come up with." No, she realized as the flatness in his eyes sharpened. What he looked was scared. "I mean, not that I care one way or the other. I'm just curious."

One corner of his mouth tucked up before he looked away. "Nothing to be curious about. You're reading more into it than there is." He scratched behind one ear, then squinted at her. "And when we're done, I'll be glad to let Miguel and Blue show me their trick, okay? So you can ratchet down the Mama-protecting-her-cubs thing a notch."

"This isn't about me, Eli," Tess said, unaccountably irked. "But after what Miguel's been through with his dad, he'll pick up in an instant if you're just playing nice."

"I won't be," he said, frowning at the ugly gold sink before gesturing toward the hard-water-stained tub. "You do realize this room's gonna have to be gutted, right? New tub, new toilet, the works?"

"You're changing the subject."

"No, actually I'm getting back on subject," he said, his opaque eyes at odds with the it's-all-good grin. "Which would be this house."

Fine, two could play at this, Tess thought, despite the not-so-vague dissatisfaction suddenly gnawing at her. No, more than that—an annoyance that the man was systematically annihilating her preconceived notions about his being, well, basically one-dimensional.

Like she needed layered men in her life right now.

Like she needed any man in her life right now.

"The Harrises have been warned," she said, following him out of the room and back into the kitchen, hauling Julia up into her arms when the little girl came running over to her, a multilimbed bundle of joy. "In fact—" she kissed the baby's chubby cheek, then looked back at Eli, who was giving her a strange look "—I told him flat out the scuzzy bathroom was a big reason why the place hadn't sold. Squicking out potential buyers is not the way to go. Oh, no, honey," she said when Julia launched herself toward Eli. "He doesn't want—"

But he'd caught the baby before she landed on her noggin, setting her in the curve of his arm like it was the most natural thing in the world. He didn't exactly go all goo-goo-ga-ga over her, giving her what seemed to Tess a cautious smile, but he seemed comfortable enough holding her, so she let it go.

"To tell you the truth," he said, looking back at the cabinets, "easiest thing would be to just rip 'em all out, replace 'em with standard stock from Lowe's or Home Depot or someplace. Heckuva lot cheaper, too."

"They won't *look* cheap?"

"Nah, they'll look fine. And we can do granite veneer on the counters, looks great, but for, like, a quarter of the cost of solid." He looked around. "Ditch the wallpaper, paint the walls, maybe do some tiling on the backsplash if you want…" He looked over, a slight smile tilting his lips. "I can get you an estimate by late tomorrow. How's that?"

"Um, sure, that's great—"

"Okay, pumpkin, back to your mama," he said, handing the

baby over and returning to the living room. "So, Miguel. Show how me what you taught the dog."

It was pitiful, the way the kid lit up. Pitiful and totally understandable. "Okay!" he said, bending over and patting his thighs. "C'mere, Blue! C'mere, boy!" The dog's bat ears half-lowered, he looked back at Eli as if to say, *Do I gotta?* At Eli's nod, the thing sighed and plodded over to Micky. "Now *sit!*" When the dog sat, Miguel looked at Eli, beaming. "Told you!"

Smiling, Tess glanced back at Eli just in time to catch an achy expression on his face that stopped her smile cold, even as the man chuckled. "Let's see if it works for me. Come, Blue." The dog literally rolled his eyes, heaved himself to his feet and plodded back to Eli. "Sit, Blue. Well, look at that— you're a good teacher, Miguel! Okay," he said, gathering up his things. "I gotta git, but you two be good for your mama, y'hear?" Then he boot-scooted his fine self out of there, Blue trotting along behind.

Bizarre.

And all the way home, as Miguel yammered about how cool Eli was, the whole dog-sitting incident bugged. Yeah, Eli'd done and said all the right things, but Tess couldn't shake the feeling something was off. Not that he didn't like kids, or even that he didn't know what to do with them, but…

But like there was a story there he wasn't telling.

And if she was smart, she'd let it stay untold.

Situated in what used to be an old A-frame house far enough from the center of town to be discreet, but not so far as to inconvenience anybody, the Lone Star Bar was about as threatening as a toothless hound dog. And almost as comical. Even with most of the original walls ripped out, the inside was hardly big enough for a decent-size bar, let alone the handful of tables and chairs and the requisite pool table squeezed into the back corner. Oh, and the six-foot-square "stage" set up for karaoke night. Ramon Viera, the owner, used to joke the place was so small he didn't dare hire chesty waitresses for fear they'd put somebody's eye out. But if, like Eli, you just wanted someplace to de-stress for a few minutes, there was no place better.

Ramon's bushy eyebrows barely lifted when Eli slid onto one of the dozen barstools. "Hey, Eli…haven't seen you in forever," he said over Reba McIntyre's warbling on the juke-box, the clacking of billiard balls, some gal's high-pitched laugh. "Everything okay?"

Hell, no. Not by a long shot. And all it'd taken was the feel of Tess's little girl in his arms, the yearning in a six-year-old boy's eyes, for everything he'd worked so hard to put behind him to come roaring back up in his face, just like that.

"What? I can't stop in for old times' sake?"

Ramon shrugged. And grinned. Took a lot more than a cranky carpenter to offend the old bartender. "What'll it be?"

"Whatever's on tap," Eli said, tossing a couple bucks on the pock-marked bar when Ramon placed the filled glass in front of him, only to nearly choke on a cloud of perfume pungent enough to spray crops with.

"Well, hello, stranger," Suze Jenkins said, sliding up onto the seat beside him. "How 'bout buying a girl a drink?"

Oh, Lord. They'd gone out exactly once, probably five years ago, although Eli couldn't for the life of him remember why. What he did remember was that a) nothing had happened, and b) Suze had been right pissed about that. That despite his calling the next day to say he was sorry, but it didn't seem right to leave her dangling when he knew nothing was gonna blossom between them—which had seemed the decent thing to do, if you asked him—she'd been harder to shake than a burr off a long-furred dog. And although she eventually let go, she still occasionally popped up, just seeing if the wind had changed.

"Not sure that's a good idea," Eli now said, taking a sip of his beer, eyes straight ahead.

"Chicken."

Finally, he looked at Tess's business partner, seeing exactly what he'd seen then—a pretty woman in a low-cut sweater with desperation issues as strong as her perfume. "Just not in the mood for misinterpretations, that's all."

"Oh, come on…after all this time? Don't make me laugh." She signaled to Ramon, ordered a whiskey and soda. "Heard you might be doing some work on the Coyote Trail house," she said after Ramon set her drink in front of her.

Eli frowned. "How'd you find that out?"

"Candy might have mentioned it…oh, crap," she said as she knocked her purse off the counter, adding, "No, that's okay, I'll get it," when she bent over, a move that bathed her ample cleavage in a deep, neon-red glow.

"Nothing's set in stone yet," Eli muttered, looking away. "Not until I submit my bid to the Harrises."

Once more upright, Suze fluffed her streaky bangs and took a sip of her drink. "And good luck with that. Tightwads."

Unaccountably irritated, Eli said, "Tess already got 'em to agree to a budget of about twenty grand. Long as I come in under that, we're good."

"Even so…" Suze dunked her swizzle stick between her ice cubes. "How Tess thinks she can move that place is beyond me. Especially by Christmas? No way. I mean, if I couldn't make it happen, nobody can."

"And maybe you shouldn't be so sure about that," Eli said, glancing toward the door just as his younger brother Noah came through it. Thinking, *Thank You, Lord,* Eli muttered his excuses, leaving another couple of bills on the counter to cover Suze's drink before grabbing his beer and crossing to meet his brother.

"Talk about your perfect timing," he said in a low voice.

Noah chuckled. "Yeah, you might want to watch out for that one." He settled into a wooden chair at a hubcap-size table, tossing his cowboy hat on it and ruffling his short, light brown hair. "She's like Super Glue."

"The new and improved formula," Eli said, dropping into the other chair and shoving the hat aside to make room for his beer, wondering what it was about the west that made so many men who'd never gone near a cow don the duds. Himself included. Then he realized what Noah'd said. "You and Suze…?"

"Couple years ago. In my 'older woman' phase. Waaiit a minute…you, too?"

"Woman's got one hell of a gravitational pull," Eli said on a rough sigh. "Wasn't serious, though. Least, not on my part."

Leaning back, his brother barked out a laugh. "When have you ever been serious? About anybody?"

"Look who's talking," Eli said, smoothly shifting the conversation away from himself. Away from the memories being around Tess had provoked, about a period in his life his younger brothers didn't know about, when Eli thought he'd finally gotten a handle on *serious* and *responsible,* only to discover he didn't know jack.

Oblivious, Noah grinned, then crossed his arms. "Actually, I'm glad I ran into you. Since I've been meaning to call anyway."

"We see each other every damn day, what—?"

"It's about Silas. Mom's about to drive him nuts."

"Mom drives all of us nuts, it's what she does," Eli said with an indulgent smile. "What about this time?"

"From what I could tell, she's seriously on his case about how he needs to move past Lori, start looking around for a new mother for the boys, how it's too hard, him raising two babies on his own." Noah grimaced. "You know how she gets."

Didn't he just? However… "The boys aren't babies anymore. Tad's, what? Three now?"

"And Ollie's in kindergarten, I know. But far as Mom's concerned, long as they have baby teeth, they're still babies. And there's something unnatural about men raising babies by themselves."

"Silas is a big boy. I imagine he can handle Mom just fine."

"He also doesn't want to hurt her feelings, not after how bad Dad and her felt when his marriage bit the dust. No, I'm serious," he added when Eli shook his head. "Silas told me he went to pick up the boys the other day, and Sally Perkins was there."

Swallowing, Eli set down his beer. "From church, Sally Perkins?"

"The very one. Now you know that's just twelve kinds of wrong. So I thought maybe you and me could, I don't know, run interference or something."

"No."

"Bro. *Sally Perkins.*"

Yeah, Mom must be getting pretty desperate if she was flinging Sally Perkins at his brother. And Mom desperate was not a pretty picture. "Okay, fine," Eli said on a released breath. "I'll think of something. But if Si finds out, you do realize he'll kill us, right?"

"Can't be worse than the torture he inflicted on us when we were younger," Noah said, and Eli chuckled. Hard to remember their geeky brother's hellion phase. Minute he had his first kid it was like he became a new person. A better person, Eli thought with a trace of bitterness. Man, what was up with the past being all up in his face tonight?

"Does Dad know?" he asked. "About Mom?"

His younger brother shook his head. "If he does, he's probably on her side. You know how they always go on about wanting us to have what they've had. But it's even worse for Silas, with the two boys and all. Why she can't see he's okay, I have no idea."

"Okay, tell you what," Eli said as Noah's cell phone rang. "If the opportunity arises, I'll broach the subject with Dad. Although like you say, they're usually on the same side about everything, so don't expect any miracles."

Although, frankly, he thought as his brother answered the call, what he'd say to his father, he had no idea. Not that he'd wish his mother's well-intentioned nagging—let alone Sally Perkins—on anybody, but the fact was Silas was anything but "okay." Something about all the mornings he'd come in to do the accounts—late—looking like hell warmed over because one kid or the other had been up sick half the night, or just that frazzled look from trying to keep the several dozen plates he had going at any one time from all crashing down on his head.

The thing was, much as it killed Eli to admit it, Mom rarely meddled without cause. *Good* cause. And the second thing was, call him old-fashioned, but in this case maybe she was right, even if her *modus operandi* could use a little tweaking. Not that Eli didn't know plenty of single parents who did a bang-up job of raising their kids on their own, but in his brother's case, the strain was definitely showing.

Just like it was with Tess, he thought with a spurt of annoyance. And something like sympathy. Maybe that's what was bugging him about her—the way she seemed so determined to show everybody how much she had her act together when it was patently obvious she was coming apart at the seams. To him, anyway. Oh, sure, if anybody could keep a hundred plates up in the air at once, it would be Tess, but that'd been one helluva meltdown she'd had that night. Pretty good indication things weren't nearly as okay in Tessville as she wanted everyone to believe.

And why Eli cared, he had no idea. Proving to her he'd grown up was one thing. But this insane urge to take care of her? After what he'd been through? No damn way—

"Yo, Eli…where'd you go, guy?"

Took him a second for his brother's face to come into focus.

"Just thinking about the bid I need to be working on," Eli said, swallowing the last of his beer and getting to his feet.

"Bid? What bid?"

"Charley's house is back on the market. Needs some updating. Dad's busy, so I signed on."

"No kidding? Fred and Gilly sellin' the place on their own?"

"No. Tess Montoya's the agent."

Noah frowned. "Didn't you used to—?"

"Shut up," Eli grunted, his brother's evil laugh following him as he wormed his way through the noisy crowd to get the hell out of there.

## Chapter Six

Kisses duly dispensed—how long, Tess wondered, before Miguel called a halt to that?—she sat in the drop-off zone in front of the elementary school, leaning farther and farther over to watch her little boy run off to join his classmates on the playground, until some doofus behind her leaned on his horn.

*Okay, so maybe I'm just a smidgen overprotective,* she thought as she pulled away, Julia singing one of her tuneless creations behind her. Tess suddenly had a vision of her baby with a nose ring and pink hair up on a stage somewhere surrounded by drugged-out rockers and nearly had a heart attack.

"Birdies, Mama! Look!" the little girl cried as they passed a naked ash tree studded with big, black, scary-looking crows. One of them cawed; Julia cawed right back, then giggled, and Tess relaxed, deciding she probably had a few years yet to worry about her daughter's induction into the dark side. Right now, her major concern was getting the kid to her babysitter's so Tess and Eli could trek to Home Depot to choose cabinets and paint and such.

Yeah, she was so looking forward to that. Sitting next to him in the confined space of somebody's vehicle. For a half hour. Each way. Smelling him. Hearing him—

*Please, God, just don't let him chuckle, 'kay? Thanks.*

It'd been a week since the Harrises approved Eli's bid, bless their miserly souls, wrenching from Tess a promise she'd do an open house the Saturday after Thanksgiving. Never mind that open houses right before Christmas were pretty much nonstarters. Because people were, you know, doing Christmas shopping and putting up trees and wrapping presents and who the hell went house shopping in December?

Not that she used those exact words.

And anyway, these days grasping at straws was better than grasping at nothing. Maybe.

At least the demolition phase was moving along nicely. And quickly. Eli had found worker bees from God knew where—cousins and brothers and uncles of the guys who worked in the shop, she gathered—and lo and behold, the '60s were vanishing right before her eyes. Now all the gutted kitchen needed was new cabinets and counters to make it all purdy—not to mention inhabitable—and they'd be good to go. But since the Harrises had entrusted Tess with all the design decisions—as in, as long as the project came in on time and under budget, they didn't give a rat's booty what it looked like—Eli insisted Tess go with him to help choose.

Hence her rumbly tummy.

She pulled up in front of the tidy little ranch-style house where Carmen Alvarado, Evangelista's niece and Tess's part-time babysitter, lived. One of her own toddlers straddling her hip, the smiling, slightly pudgy young woman opened her door, calling to Julia in Spanish before Tess had fully untangled her from her car seat. It wasn't that the area locals couldn't speak English—most of them did, as well or better than their gringo counterparts. But if English was a pair of dress shoes worn only in company, Spanish was that favorite pair of slippers you put on as soon as you got home.

Except for Tess, whose mother had refused to let her speak Spanish growing up, or even to take it in school, a quirk—the nicest word Tess could think of—that had always made Tess feel like part of her was missing.

Julia wriggled free as soon as the car door slammed shut, running up to her sitter, babbling about birds. *"Vi parajos, Carmen! Muchos parajos! En arbol!"*

*"Usted hizo?* Cool! *Ahora dé a su mama un beso,* sweetie!"

And wouldn't that frost Julia's grandmother? Tess thought as she and her daughter exchanged a dozen kisses before the little girl gleefully stomped up the few steps into the uber-babyproofed house filled with toys and dolls and books and healthy snacks…and no TV.

Yeah, maybe she shouldn't think too hard about Carmen's extraordinary child-care skills. "I should be back no later than two," she said, and the young woman smiled.

"No problem. Since she takes her nap from one to three, take your time."

As she was saying.

Twenty minutes later, some radio talk show—*en espanol,* natch—spilled through the half-open front door when Tess arrived at the house. Devoid of the rotting blue window trim, the house now looked like that old woman without any make-up at all, mouth and eyes agape in shock. Inside, the noise was as thick as the dust—bursts of laughter, the *pow! pow! pow!* of a nail gun, that radio show.

"Hello!" she yelled over the din, even as she took in the remarkable progress Eli and his elves had already made. Sure, it looked like a bomb had gone off, but you can't *re*-do until you *un*-do. Not only that, but the pow-pow-powing was due to the brand-new shelving going into the living room, replacing the sorry, warped built-ins.

One of the workers noticed her and nodded, grinning. "*Buscando* Mr. Eli?"

"Yeah. Is he here?"

"In the back. He'll be out in a minute." He loaded another nail into the gun, then gestured with it toward the new shelves. "You like?"

"Very much," Tess said. "They look terrific."

"*Gracias, senora.*"

"*De nada.* I'm sorry…what's your name?"

"Teo," Eli answered, coming into the room. Smiling. Making Tess's lungs seize up. "Teo Martinez." He nodded toward both the gray-haired man and the younger one on the other side of the shelves. "And his son, Luis. I was damn lucky they were both available. Couldn't ask for a better crew."

"No, it's us who are grateful, Mr. Garrett. With the economy the way it is?" He did the in-the-tank gesture with his thumb. "Not so easy, finding construction work these days." Turning back to the shelves, he lined up the nail gun and let 'er rip. *Pow.* He glanced over his shoulder at Tess while reloading. "Las' month was the firs' time in twenty-five years I have to go on unemployment. Luis, he's been laid off, what? Three, four times in the last year. With a wife and son to support, he's thinking, maybe he should join the army or the marines—"

"It's just an option, Pop," the younger man said as Tess's lungs seized again, for an entirely different reason.

"An' I tell you—" *pow* "—wait a little while, see if things pick up. An' see?" He tossed a grin in Eli's direction. "They did."

Tess's gaze slid to Eli, exchanging an apologetic glance

with the younger Martinez, and Tess guessed that this job was at best only a reprieve. The younger man shrugged—*It's okay, man, I'm cool*—then bestowed a beautiful smile on Tess that broke her heart.

At that moment, Eli wasn't sure what was tearing him up more—Luis's bravado or the obvious turmoil that bravado provoked in Tess. Because even though she was smiling and commending Luis for wanting to serve his country, Eli could tell the conversation was bringing a whole lot of junk to the surface…even if he couldn't immediately identify what that junk was.

"Looks great, guys," Eli said to the two workers, then steered Tess into the gutted kitchen. "You okay?"

Caution flashed in her eyes. "Why wouldn't I be?"

"Oh, I don't know…maybe because the minute Luis brought up the military you looked like a brick had fallen on your head?"

"That obvious, huh?"

"Uh, yeah."

Watching the young man, she breathed out a sigh. "How old is he?"

"Twenty-two."

"Same age as Ricky when he first went in," she said, more to herself than Eli. "Teo said there's a kid?"

"Yeah. A little boy. Just turned one a couple weeks ago." When Tess sucked in a breath, Eli said, "Tess? What is it?"

After several seconds, she shook her head. "Nothing. You ready to go?"

"Sure," Eli said slowly, grabbing a leather baseball jacket off the counter's skeleton and shrugging into it. He fished his car keys out of his pants pocket, then patted his other pockets, sighing. "Okay, I'm an idiot, I must've left my wallet at the shop."

"It's okay, we can take my car. I just gassed up, anyway."

"That's fine, but I need the company credit card. Which is in my wallet—"

"Wait—you've been driving without your license?"

"Yeah. From the shop to here. And since I wasn't giving the sheriff any reason to pull me over, you can wipe that oh-my-God-you-didn't look off your face. But you mind if we swing by the shop on our way out of town?"

"Not at all," Tess said. Looking highly amused.

He told the guys they'd be back in a couple of hours, then followed Tess outside and to her car, not realizing until his hand landed on the driver door handle what he was doing. As he trooped around to the passenger side, grumbling, Tess laughed. It wasn't the old Tess laugh—the laugh that used to drive him crazy, in a good way—but then, this wasn't the old Tess.

"It must be killing you," she said as they both got in, "letting me drive. You couldn't stand it..." The key in the ignition, her eyes darted to his. "Before."

"What can I say? I've evolved." Shoulder belt latched, Eli leaned back, watching her. "At least, on the surface." When she gave him a puzzled look, he shrugged. "It's not like letting a woman drive threatens my masculinity or something. But to tell you the truth...sitting on this side of the car? I hate it. If I'm in a vehicle, I want to be the one driving. The one making the decisions that could mean the difference between me being alive at the end of the trip or not." At her silence, he glanced over. "Just bein' honest."

Her mouth twitching, she glanced at him. "Can't very well take offence since I feel exactly the same way."

"Now why doesn't that surprise me?"

"You think this means we have control issues?"

"Oh, I know we do," he said. Then grinned. "Especially you."

She didn't grin back. Although she didn't try smacking

him with her purse, either. So he'd count that as a draw. "How on earth I'll ever teach the kids to drive, though, I have no idea."

"This is why God made driver's ed. And you need to turn right up ahead—"

"I know where I'm going, Eli. Sheesh."

But at least she was smiling.

When they got to the shop, Eli said, "You may as well come in. This might take a while."

"You don't know where your wallet is?"

"Sure I do. It's in there. Somewhere."

Rolling her eyes, she got out of the car and followed him inside. Jose glanced up from the table saw, nodding to Tess as she followed Eli back to his workspace. "Wow," she said when she noticed the headboard. "That's amazing. Who's it for?"

"A client who canceled his order."

"Idiot," she muttered, then walked over to get a closer work. "Thea told me you'd gone into furniture making, but I had no idea you were this talented. No, seriously, I'm impressed. And I don't impress easily." *Now there's a shock,* Eli thought as she added, "What're you going to do with it?"

"Haven't decided yet," Eli muttered, pawing through the crap on his workbench.

"Wait a minute…I'd planned on staging the house anyway—if you haven't sold the bed by the first open house, could I borrow it?"

Eli looked over. "You serious?"

"Absolutely. I've still got the old queen mattress and boxsprings in my garage from when I changed out the master bedroom…" She shut her eyes for a second, then said, "And I'm sure I can rustle up a comforter and some pillows. And who knows, maybe somebody will buy it. So how about it?"

"Well…okay, then. Yeah. Thanks." Eli spotted the shirt

jacket he'd been wearing the day before; sure enough, the wallet was in the chest pocket.

"Any other furniture just lying around?" Tess said, craning her neck.

"Sorry, no. Although…" He glanced over at a stack of reclaimed lumber he'd been hoarding for more than a year. "I might be able to throw together a dining table and a couple of benches. If that would work."

"Oh, don't go to any extra trouble—"

"I wouldn't be." He held up the wallet. "Got it. Ready?"

As they traipsed back front, though, she stopped for a moment to chat with Jose—apparently his son and Enrique had been in boot camp together—and something warm bloomed inside him as Eli realized her friendliness wasn't some salesperson schtick, but stemmed from a genuine concern about how other people were getting on. Not that she couldn't get as bristly as the next person, if the situation—or the offense—warranted it. But neither did she let cynicism infect her relationships.

Not all of them anyway.

"Teo clearly thinks the world of you," she said once they were on the road again. "For giving him and Luis work."

"Just glad this job came along so I could. We've known the family forever. Mom and Teo's wife, Luisa, do a lot of church stuff together."

"Here," she said, fishing a small pad and pen out of her purse on the console between them as she drove one-handed. Eli nearly had a stroke. "Write down their number," she said, wagging them at him. "In case I hear of any other work in the area."

Eli pulled out his cell, clicking through his contacts menu until he found Luis's number. As he wrote it down, he slid his eyes to Tess. "Please tell me you're not one of those women who puts on her makeup while driving."

"Dear God, no," she said on a short laugh. "Ricky hated that—" She hissed in a quick breath. "Sorry. Sometimes I forget. That he's not really part of my life anymore."

Replacing the pad and pen in her purse, Eli said, "Does it bother you to talk about him?"

A shrug preceded, "Depends on the day. Sometimes, yeah. Sometimes not." She shoved a tuft of hair behind her ear; it popped right back out. "Since there's nobody to talk *to,* though, it's kinda moot."

"What about your aunt? Or your friends?"

They drove probably another half mile or so before she quietly said, "Dumping on the people you care about gets old real fast."

"Even though you'd do the same for them."

She shot him a glance. "And you know this how?"

"Because I know—or knew, at any rate—you. In school, you were always the sounding board for everybody else, the guys, as well as the girls. It was weird," he said when she softly laughed. "So how is it everybody can bitch to you, but you don't feel right about letting somebody else bear the burden from time to time?"

Her hands tightened around the steering wheel. At perfect ten-to-two driving school formation. "Maybe because I don't feel I need to, because I'm doing okay—"

"Like hell," he said, and her eyes flashed to his. "I was there, Tess," he said when she looked away, her mouth set in an angry line. "People who're 'okay' don't have wild sex with their old boyfriends."

"And I could've gone all day without you bringing that up."

"It happened, Tess. You can't deny it. And God knows I'm not gonna. And it seems to me maybe you better figure out *why* it happened. Because if the earth tilts on its axis and we ever do that again, I wanna make good and sure it's not because you're mad at the world and taking it out on me."

"If we ever…?" Her laugh this time was sharp. "I can't believe you said that."

"Just saying, if it does."

"Well, it's not. So you can put that thought right out of your head." She paused. "And I thought you didn't care. About my…" Her lips smushed together. "Motivation."

"That time, no. Just don't let it become a habit."

"Oh, for heaven's sake, Eli—" When he chuckled, she realized she'd been had. "I hate you," she said, without heat.

"Ah…just like old times," he said, propping one boot on the dashboard, earning a disapproving frown. "Do I make you nervous?"

Her head whipped around so fast her sunglasses slipped. "What? No!" When he raised one eyebrow, she released a breath. "Okay, maybe a little—"

"Ha!"

Her mouth turned down at the corners. "It's…strange being around you again. That's all."

"You can say that again," Eli said nonchalantly, slouching down as much as the seat belt would let him, his hands folded over his stomach.

"Do I…make *you* nervous?"

"Heck, yeah. 'Cause it's like I should know you, you know? Only I don't. And yet…"

"What?"

He looked at her. "Before, when we were kids? I know ninety, maybe ninety-five percent of the relationship was about body contact. But the five to ten percent that wasn't?" Focusing back out the windshield, he said, "I really liked you, Tess. Hell, I thought you were the coolest person I'd ever known."

"Oh, God, Eli—"

"Don't go getting your panties in a twist. I'm not tryin' to score or anything. Exactly." He ducked, chuckling, when one hand flew over the gearshift to smack at him. "But I guess what I'm trying to say is, some tiny part of that—it's still alive. On my side of the fence anyway. I mean, by rights, this should feel totally bizarre, right? After all those years apart, then us hooking up like that." He waited for another sputtering explosion that never happened. "And yet in some ways this feels completely natural. Which is what makes it so weird." He sighed. "Am I making any sense at all?"

The Home Depot in their sights, she met his eyes. "Yeah. You are." Turning into the parking lot, she added, "Which only goes to show how bad off *I* am."

However, once in the store, Tess impressed the hell out of him by charging straight to the cabinet section, no veering off down aisles they didn't need to be. And within maybe thirty seconds of his showing her the few options that were not only in stock, but within their meager budget, she said, "That one. See you in Paint," and off she went, leaving him to order what they needed. Not surprisingly, by the time he caught up with her in the paint department, the first of four different colors were being mixed up.

Leaning against the paint counter, Eli softly laughed.

"What's so funny now?"

"Just never met a gal who didn't prevaricate for a week about choosing paint colors. Took my mom three months to decide what color to repaint the living room, another month to choose the carpet to go with it."

"And you're basing all women on that one experience?"

"Nope. My ex-sister-in-law was just as bad. And there might've been a girlfriend or two along the way who'd watched one too many episodes on HGTV who'd dragged me shopping with her. Drove me nuts. Me, I point to something, say, 'Yeah, that one,' and that's it. Half makes me wonder if you're really a woman."

Tess gave him a look. Eli grinned harder.

"So," she said, moving smartly along, "you got close enough to a 'girlfriend or two' to do the decorating thing?"

"Not by choice, believe me." He paused. "And that pretty much signaled the end of those relationships, too."

"Death by paint chips?"

"You wanna send a man to hell, show him fifteen different shades of white and ask him which one he likes better."

Tess laughed, and Eli smiled, thinking, *Don't stop.* The dude clunked the first two gallons up on the counter, went to work on the next batch. "I'm not a ditherer. Especially when it's not for me," she said, skimming a finger along one can's rim. A beat or two passed before she looked back at him. "And I've learned the sorts of colors more likely lead to an offer. Warm neutrals," she said, holding up a swatch that reminded him of coffee with too much cream.

A few feet away, a couple started bickering with each other in Spanish. Figuring it wasn't exactly a private affair, Eli didn't even pretend not to listen in. Except they were talking too fast for him to pick out more than a word here and there. He nudged Tess with his elbow. "What're they saying?" he whispered.

"What?" she said, then glanced over her shoulder. Shaking her head, she turned back to her paint swatches. "Something about his mother, but that's about all I can make out. My Spanish is from hunger, remember?"

"Why is that?"

She shrugged. "Mom never let me speak it. She considered it low class. What do you think of this for the dining room?" she said, holding up another swatch.

"It's…yellow? And what do you mean your mother considered it low class?"

"Just what I said. Not a whole lot of Latino love goin' on in my house growing up. And can we please change the subject?"

He got the message. "You got a painter lined up?"

"Yeah. Me."

"You?"

Again with the eyes. "I painted my whole house myself. I imagine I'll be okay with a few accent walls and a bathroom. And it'll help stay within the budget." Grunting softly, she hefted first one can, then the other into the cart. "I've become very handy over the years, I'll have you know."

"You one of those gals who changes her own tires?"

"One of my least favorite jobs in the world, but yep. And my oil, sparkplugs and filters, too."

"Impressive."

"Not at all. Just easier than depending on someone else," she said as the next can of paint appeared in front of them. Eli grabbed it before she did, if for no other reason than to avoid the strange look the paint-mixer dude was giving him. Maybe because Tess weighed less than the paint.

Forty-five minutes later—after choosing the cabinet hardware, backsplash tile and bathroom vanity and fixtures with equal efficiency—they were back in her SUV and Eli realized he was starving.

"Hey. Wanna burger or something? My treat."

"I can buy my own lunch—"

"I'm sure you can, but you're not gonna today. So deal. So what'll it be? Mickey D's, Wendy's or Burger King?"

"I think my arteries just screamed."

"You don't eat meat?"

"Meat that doesn't look like it's been run over by a steamroller, sure. If something's gonna eventually kill me, I'd at least like to enjoy the process." Her mouth worked for a second before she abruptly turned off the highway onto a little street winding away from the touristy area. "You want a burger, I'll show you a *burger.*"

Twenty minutes later, Eli grinned down at a burger so fat and juicy and sassy he half expected it to moo. Then he looked over at Tess, her eyes closed as she savored her own first bite, and something squeezed tight in his chest.

"I take it," he said, "you haven't had one of these in a while, either."

Tess shot him a look, but was apparently too caught up in red meat worship to make a comeback. Swallowing, she shook her head. "Taking two little kids someplace like this is a waste. One bite and they're done. Or have to go potty. Sure, the girls and I have our Ortega's Wednesdays—sometimes— but it's not the same as—"

Lowering her burger to her plate, she turned toward the window. But not before Eli saw tears swell in her eyes.

"Hey," he said, dipping his head. "You okay?"

"I'm fine," she said on an embarrassed half laugh, then pressed the edge of her napkin to one eye. "Have no idea where that came from. Don't take it personally."

"Wouldn't dream of it."

"No, I mean…" She blew out a breath, then took a sip of her iced tea. "I'd just forgotten how nice it can be to have a civilized meal. Even if it's just a burger and fries. Just two adults sitting in a booth…" She shook her head, laughing a little.

Covering.

"Hey," Eli said, and she looked up again, chewing. "Admitting you enjoy the company of somebody over four feet tall isn't a sign of weakness. Even if the company is me. Although I'm flattered as hell you consider me an adult."

He'd expected—wanted—a laugh. Instead, she lowered her gaze again, dunking a French fry in a pool of ketchup for several seconds before answering. "Okay, confession time… watching you work, the way you interact with your crew…" She almost smiled. "Whatever personal baggage we have between us, I can't deny the person I've seen over the past couple of weeks…"

Eli went completely still, watching her. Waiting. Finally she lifted her eyes, looking seriously put out with herself. "I was wrong about you, okay? And seeing somebody for who he is— not who you thought he was—has nothing to do with flattery."

Wow. Talk about your whoa and damn moments. Eli leaned back, one arm stretched across the booth seat's top. "Despite all the gossip?"

Her mouth flattened. "My mother's been on my mind a lot lately for some reason. Like a rash that comes and goes," she added wryly. "You know what they say about a woman putting on a coat and her mother's arm coming out of the sleeve? Being around you…it's made me remember when I decided to never get anywhere near that coat if I could help it. About the time you and I met, actually."

"I'm not following."

She sighed. "My mother was—still is—hugely judgmental. Hardly anybody ever meets her standards. It's all about the surface with her. But living with that attitude is like being around secondhand smoke. After a while, you don't notice it, realize that it's poisoning you, too. And if somebody hurts you, the poison leaches out, sometimes without you even knowing it." She hmmphed out a soft laugh. "Brother, can I murder a metaphor or what?"

"It's okay, I got it. Mostly."

"What I'm trying to say is…sometimes I forget whose daughter I am, and I fall into the trap of judging without really seeing. So. I apologize."

"I'm officially off your jerk list?"

"For the moment," she said, sorta smiling.

Eli took a swallow of his tea and ventured, "Does your mom's…"

"Craziness?"

"Whatever. Did that it have something to do with your dad's leaving?"

Tess munched on another fry for a moment, her brow knotted. "I don't know. I was so little when he left, I don't remember the details. They didn't fight, that I can recall. Maybe she froze him out with her indifference? Of course, we're talking about a man who never contacted his only child again." She squinted out the window. "He died a couple of years ago."

"I didn't know, I'm sorry." She shrugged. "How'd you find out?"

"Mom told me. Some months after the fact. 'Oh, by the way,'" she said, mimicking her mother's high-pitched voice to a T, "'your father's brother wrote to tell me Tom had passed.'"

"Tact not being your mother's strong suit."

She made a funny sound in her throat. "There's an understatement. Seeing as she also said I was a mistake. Oh, God, listen to me, doing exactly what I—"

"To your face?"

When her mouth flattened, Eli leaned across the table to close his fingers around her wrist. "Honey, it's generally not a good idea to keep the poison inside. Especially once it's started leaking, anyway. And it's not like I'm gonna tell anybody, if that's what's worrying you—"

"No!" she said, all wide-eyed. "That never even occurred to me!"

"Good," Eli said, letting go to pick up another French fry, which he waved in her direction. "So? How did you find out?"

For a few seconds he thought for sure she was going to ignore him. Then she finally said, "I overheard her on the phone with someone. Aunt Flo, maybe."

"Damn," Eli said when the rushing in his ears settled down. "How old were you?"

"Not sure. Pretty young. Still in elementary school."

"You never told me. Back then, I mean."

"Talking wasn't exactly a top priority. Back then."

"Good point," he said, then folded his arms. "Maybe she didn't really mean it?"

That got a smirk. "One day I decided to ask her. Stupidest thing I've ever done. Okay, *second* stupidest thing I've ever done," she added when he snorted. "Anyway, instead of denying it, or even trying to cover her butt, all she said was 'I did the best I knew how by you, Teresa. You can't expect any more from me than that.'"

"That's terrible."

"And you wonder why there's no love lost between us."

"Not anymore, I don't. Damn, Tess, if I'd had any idea… maybe I would've handled things differently."

She frowned. "And maybe I didn't say anything because I didn't want you to stay with me out of pity."

Eli didn't have to ask her if that's what made her hesitate before, what made her loathe to bitch about her problems in general, because she didn't want anybody to feel sorry for her. Man, he could only imagine the number her mother must've done on her head…and the inner strength it had taken to overcome it.

"A person would be hard put to see you as a victim," he said softly, and her eyes darted to his. He shrugged. "Just sayin'. But you know, as much as my folks drive all of us crazy with the meddling and the worryin' and all of that, hearing you talk about your mother…I'll never complain about mine again."

Tess smiled. "Yes, you will."

"Yeah, probably. But I'll think twice before I do. Damn, Tess, I'm sorry. I guess I chalked up your issues with your mom to, you know, the normal teenager daughter-mother stuff. I had no idea it was that bad."

"Neither did I, to be honest. Because she wasn't mean or anything. Just, like I said…indifferent. Like I was a plant someone had left for her to take care of while they went on vacation. Forget trying to get her approval, I could barely get her *attention*. So I finally gave up." Her shoulders hitched as she swept a fry through what was left of her ketchup puddle. Then she smiled, barely meeting his gaze. "It sometimes amazes me I didn't turn out more screwed up than I am."

"I just don't get…" Eli's hand fisted around his napkin. "How a mother could do that to her own kid." He paused. "How anyone could do that to *you*."

Her eyes darkened for a moment before she shrugged again. "Whatever her reasons, I decided the dysfunction buck stopped with me. That no way was I passing on that particular legacy to my kids. They will know…" She cleared her throat. "They will always know they're loved, that I wanted them. That I want them *around*. And that they come first and always will."

"Good for you," Eli said over the unexpected, and uncalled for, sting. "I gotta ask, though—did you take up with me in high school because you knew it would frost your mother?"

Tess's laugh was so sharp heads turned. Pressing her napkin to her mouth, she shook her head. "No," she said, lowering it. "At least, not consciously. Although she certainly wasn't amused."

"So I remember."

"It's weird…she'd hardly acknowledge my presence for months, then she'd suddenly realize, oh, crap—when was the last time I watered that plant? Like I'd come out of my room dressed for school and she'd scowl and tell me I looked like a dork. Or a slut," she muttered.

"Trust me, you never looked like a slut."

"Thanks. I didn't think so, either, but…" Tess sighed. "When I started going with you was one of those phases—suddenly nobody was good enough for her precious daughter. She didn't exactly jump for joy when I got engaged to Enrique, either. Although she had no problem with the 'Didn't I tell yous?' when it fell apart, either. Now that she's bagged her gringo Texan rancher, though, I suppose she's finally happy—"

Her phone rang. She dug it out of her purse, frowning at the display. "Yes?…Oh!" Her fingers tightened around the phone. "Yes, of course…I'll be right there—I mean, I'll be there as soon as I can. I'm in Santa Fe…yes, thank you for calling."

Eli had already signaled for the check by the time Tess got off the phone, so frantic to leave she bumped into the waitress when she stood, muttering her apologies before streaking toward the front.

He handed the girl a twenty, signaling he didn't need anything back, then scurried to catch up. "That was Micky's school," Tess said, shoving open the door and stomping to the car. "He got hurt at recess—what are you doing?"

"Driving," Eli said, taking the keys from her.

"But—"

"No way am I putting my life in the hands of someone shaking as badly as you are right now. So just get in and let's go, okay?"

Amazingly, she didn't argue.

## Chapter Seven

*Don't freak, don't freak, don't—*

"Omigod," Tess said under her breath at her first glimpse of her baby through the glass wall separating the nurse's office from the school's reception area. The nurse had already warned her that Micky—sitting forlornly on the edge of a cot—was pretty banged up, even though he was basically okay. Now, seeing the result of tender little face meeting asphalt, Tess clasped her hand over her mouth to hold in the gasp.

"You should probably go in," Eli said, his hand at the small of her back.

"I know," she said, perilously close to the edge of an emotional cliff. Bad enough she'd started gabbing to Eli about her mother, dredging up all sorts of unpleasantness, but now this? Tears pushed at her eyes; she forced them to retreat through sheer willpower.

"Come on," Eli said, opening the door. Steering her. Taking charge.

Pushing her closer to the edge of that cliff even as he pushed her into the nurse's office.

"Hey, buddy," he said softly, giving Tess a chance to find her voice. Micky's head shot up. "Heard you had a little accident."

Eyes bright with tears, his lower lip quivering, he nodded.

"What happened, baby?" Tess said, moving to take him in her arms, but he dodged her hug.

"I was runnin' and tripped."

"Somebody's still a little in shock," the nurse said, giving Micky's shoulder a quick squeeze. "Unfortunately, no matter how vigilant the duty teachers are, playground accidents sometimes happen. The good news is, it looks a lot worse than it is. We got it all cleaned up, but it's not bad enough to put a dressing on. Besides, it'll scab over and heal more quickly that way. So just keep it clean, and if he wants to stay home for a couple of days I'm sure everyone will understand. You can go ahead and sign him out," she said, then smiled for the child. "You've been very brave, Miguel. Your parents should be very proud of you."

This with a smile for Eli. Oops.

Her heart slowly retreating from her throat, Tess followed Eli and Micky out of the nurse's office, trying once more to hug him before she signed him out. Again, he pulled away, refusing to let her comfort him.

Her heart aching, Tess glanced at Eli. *Is this a boy thing I don't know about?*

"It's okay," he mouthed. Then, louder, "Go on, we'll wait right here."

Before she got to the desk, however, she heard Eli say in a low voice, "You know, I'm bettin' your mama could really use a hug right now."

"How come?"

"To make her feel better."

"But I'm the one who got hurt."

"I know. But she's the one who got scared."

Out of the corner of her eye, Tess caught Micky's frown. "You sure she needs a hug?"

"Oh, I'd bet my life on it."

Her signature barely recognizable because the stupid sign-out sheet went all blurry on her, Tess turned just as Micky's arms wrapped around her waist, pressing the uninjured side of his face into her stomach.

She looked up, her gaze running smack-dab into Eli's, and he gave her an A-OK sign and a smile, and her stomach went all fizzy and fluttery on her, and she thought, *Oh, hell, no, I am* so *not falling for this guy.*

Except she so was.

Then, on the way out to the car they passed a glass display case, as bad as a mirror. Before Tess could shuttle Micky past it, the little boy turned…and gasped. Eli bent beside him, his hand on his shoulder.

"Dude…I didn't want to say anything in front of your mother," he said in a stage whisper, "but you look seriously awesome."

"Huh?"

"Check it out—you look just like a zombie or something—"

"Eli, for heaven's sake—"

"Yeah?" Micky said, suddenly much more cheerful. "Cool!"

Over her son's head, Tess shot Eli a look. He shrugged, grinning, and the fizzing got so bad it almost made her sick.

Tess jerked awake from a weirdly disturbing dream in which she was a hot dog, suffocating inside the bun.

Behind her—as in, plastered right up against her back-side—Miguel snored. And against her stomach, Julia's Pull-Up'ed butt wiggled. *Good thing I'm* not *looking for a husband,* Tess thought as she extricated herself from assorted offspring, *'cause there'd be no room for him in the bed anyway.*

If that was supposed to cheer her up, it didn't. Partly because her treacherous, half-asleep brain immediately conjured up the image of a grinning, naked, aroused Eli in that bed—without the kids, obviously—partly because she still hadn't gotten over how deftly he'd handled Miguel after the playground mishap three days before.

Her stomach fizzed just thinking about it.

The groan tried desperately to escape when she bent over to search for her slippers, one only partially due to her Eli musings. Okay, she thought as the muscles in her lower back shrieked, maybe she was overdoing the painting just a tad.

Fervently hoping the kids would stay asleep long enough for the shower massage to beat the tar out of her, Tess Frankensteined it out to the hall and smacked at the thermostat, then into the bathroom, where she—stupidly—caught her reflection. At least the electric-socket hair distracted from the hamster pouches under her eyes.

Mourning her lost youth, or something, she lurched into the toilet closet, peed, then to the shower, and turned it on, emitting a rapturous sigh when steam billowed forth like a thousand gentle hands, beckoning. Caressing. Promising miracles. "Oh, yeah, baby," she murmured, shucking her nightgown—

"Mama?"

Yelping, Tess grabbed a towel off the rack and wrapped it around her, frowning at her son. Who hadn't seen her naked since he was, like, *one.* Fortunately, his lids were still at half-mast, so with any luck they weren't talking permanent trauma.

Or permanent scarring, thank God. Except for a few splotchy scabs, you could barely tell he'd looked like Two-Face a few days before.

"What are you doing up, honey? It's still real early."

"You left an' I got cold." Yawning, he trundled into the water closet and banged up the seat. "An' I'm hungry," he said over the waterfall imitation.

"Then go fix yourself a bowl of cereal," she said when he emerged. "You know how to do that. And you turn yourself right back around and flush that toilet."

Rolling his eyes, Micky stomped back, yelling, "We're all out," as he flushed.

"No, we're not."

"Yeah, we are. I looked." Underneath a bedhead only a Yeti mama could love, dark eyes brightened. "We got Teddy Grahams, though."

"Close enough." Couldn't be any worse than Apple Jacks. Still, even as she heard a sleepy, "Mama?" from the bedroom, she mentally added a double helping of broccoli to his plate that night. "And share with your sister!" she called to Miguel's back as he trudged barefoot from the room.

"On it!" he said, and Tess sputtered a laugh.

Ten steamy minutes later she was clean, dressed and—glory be—could move without looking like she was held together by rods and pins. She went into the kitchen to put on coffee, swiping a few Teddy Grahams along the way.

"Mine!" Julia bellowed, hands on hips.

"So take more," Tess said, spooning coffee into the basket, noticing Miguel had not only added string cheese to the menu but had poured them both plastic tumblers of juice. "And anyway, technically they're not yours," she said, mopping up Lake Citrus on the counter, "since I bought them. I just let you eat them 'cause I'm nice like that."

"Huh?" Miguel said as the baby frowned, then said, "I went potty!"

In the midst of rinsing out the sponge, Tess twisted around. "You did?"

"Yup," the baby said, with a curl-bouncing nod, her cheeks pooched out with bear bits, Tess assumed.

"What did you do with the Pull-Up?"

"In dere," Julia said in her adorable little whisper, pointing to the garbage.

Obsessively peeling his cheese, Child Numero Uno asked, "What's that stuff on your mouth?"

"Lipstick. Which you know." Since the kid used to beg her to wear it himself when he was three. A secret Tess would carry to the grave. "What's the big deal?"

Miguel let out a mighty sigh. "The big *deal*," he said, gesticulating like a character from "The Sopranos," "is that the funny pants look weird with the lipstick."

The funny pants being overalls. Seen-better-days, paint-spattered overalls, to be exact. The coffee gurgling to life behind her, Tess almost laughed. "You working the night shift in the Fashion Police now?"

The kid looked duly puzzled for a moment or two, then shoved another unsuspecting bear into his mouth. "It just doesn't look right. You don't look like Mama, you look like…"

*Tread carefully, little man.* "Who?"

"Like Carmen's little sister when she's going on a date."

Tess frowned. "You know what a date is?"

"Kinda. It's when a boy and girl go see a movie or get a pizza or something. Although what I don't get is, why she has to put all that junk on her face to eat pizza or sit in the dark?"

"Good point," Tess said, while, around remnants of preservative-enchanced beasties, her stomach clenched. Because the kid was right, damn his precious little hide, she had taken far more care about her makeup this morning than was necessary for *a date* with a roller and a gallon of Desert Mocha.

Oh, dear God. She was *primping?*

Tess timorously glanced at her reflection in the over-the-stove microwave, horrified to discover the lipstick had company. Hard to tell in the dark door, but unless she was mistaken she'd even gotten cozy with the concealer.

Okay, this doing-stuff-without-realizing thing was getting a *little* creepy.

"You know," she said, pouring her coffee with a slightly trembling hand, "I think maybe I'll just wash this off. I'm only gonna get paint on my face, anyway, right? So you two finish up with, um, breakfast and brush your teeth and I'll be back out in a sec, then we can get outta here—"

"Mom."

"What?"

Another dramatic sigh. "We're not dressed?"

See, this was the problem with the stomach fizzies—they also corroded your brain.

*Remember the plan where you were gonna pack up your hormones along with your wedding rings, never to be seen again? Whatever happened to that?*

Eli happened, that's what.

Barking at Miguel to find clothes, any clothes, she didn't care as long as they didn't freeze to death, Tess marched into her bathroom and washed off every single molecule of make-up. Then she smushed half a can of mousse into her hair and took the brush to it, smashing it flat and away from her face so that her ears—which she'd always hated—stuck out. Finally, satisfied she'd made herself sufficiently hideous, she tromped into the baby's room to get her dressed, taking some small satisfaction when Julia flinched and backed away until she realized it was still Mama.

*And let that be a lesson to me,* Tess thought, yanking a little purple hoodie over her daughter's head. Still Mama, only Mama…never again gonna be anything but Mama.

And no, *hot* Mama was not part of that equation.

Her landline rang. "It's Daddy!" Miguel yelled.

All those muscles she'd gotten nice and loose? Kinked right back up again.

Eli hadn't realized how shallowly he'd been breathing until he heard Tess's car pull up in front of the old house. Because Tess was never late. In fact, before this moment, he would've said Tess didn't know *how* to be late. But she'd been late this morning and it'd scared the crap out of him. Of course, now he knew she was all right, he also knew better than to let on he'd even given her lateness a second thought. None of his business what had held her up. And for damn sure he didn't have any business worrying about her.

Okay, maybe worrying might be overstating it.

Or not.

Especially when Tess stormed in through the front door like a pissed-off yellow jacket on crack, barely mumbling a greeting to the guys sanding the living room floor on her way back to the hall bathroom, which she'd been planning on painting today, and relief flooded through Eli so strong it nearly made him dizzy.

"And don't you dare follow me!" she yelled, stripping off her fleece jacket as he followed her down the hall. Good Lord, she was practically lost in those overalls. What happened to the skinny jeans? More to the point, what happened to the adorable little behind in the skinny jeans?

Not to mention everything he'd told himself about *only* wanting to make things up to her after the stunt he'd pulled way back when?

"Yeah?" he said, wading right into the quicksand anyway. "Whatcha gonna do to stop me? Beat me up?"

"Not in the mood, Eli," she said, squatting down to pry the lid off a can of light brown paint, at which point he realized—

"What the hell'd you do to your hair?"

The glare was brief, but potent. And just long enough to tell she wasn't wearing any makeup, either. Hell, woman looked like she'd had the flu for a week. Eli crouched beside her, squelching the urge to take the screwdriver from her and pop off the stubborn lid himself. Since she looked like she might bite.

"Okay, that didn't come out right—"

"No," she said on a grunt, "it came out fine. Exactly the reaction I was hoping for, actually."

Eli frowned. "Tess? Don't take this the wrong way, but you're acting really weird. Even for you." She swore when the screwdriver slipped, scraping her palm. *The hell with this,* Eli thought, grabbing both the tool and her wounded hand.

"It's *okay,* dammit!" she said, yanking free. "It's…" Her lower lip trembling—although in anger or pain or what, he couldn't tell—she lowered her butt to the bathroom tile, her back against the tub.

His stomach went into freefall. "Tess? You're not…you know. *Late* late?"

She looked up at him, her brow puckered for a moment until she pushed out a small, dry laugh. "Period came last week, right on schedule. You can breathe now."

He did, giving her a moment to collect herself—which she spent mostly by sucking on the small wound—before she mumbled, "Would you please go away?" around the base of her thumb.

"I'm thinking no," Eli said, sitting down beside her. Smelling her. *Feeling* her. Having no earthly idea what to do about any of it.

"You have work to do."

"It's not going anywhere. And neither am I." He looked over, his forehead all bunched up, thinking she was the only woman in the world who could pull off the death-warmed-over look. "But before you get started—next time you're held up, you call and let somebody know, you got that?"

That at least diverted her attention from the thumb. "Why? I don't work for you."

"I know that. But it's just…common courtesy is all. So people know you're okay."

"People," she said, her eyes boring into his. Eli looked away.

"Yeah. Like Teo and Luis and them. You know how they are. They get worried."

"I see. Then I'll be sure not to keep…Teo and them in the dark from now on."

"Good," Eli said with a sharp nod. "Now you gonna tell me what happened? You talk to your mother or something?"

She actually laughed. "No, I don't have that reaction when my mother calls. Ricky, on the other hand…"

Instantly, his insides felt like they'd been blowtorched. Why, he had no idea. The man was her ex, for crying out loud. An ex for whom she was clearly no longer pining, from the looks of things. "What'd he say to you?"

"He didn't *say* anything. Well, obviously, he did. It's just… he got on my case about Miguel, that's all, telling me I should've taken him to the E.R. after the accident, blah blah blah." She tried to run a hand through her plastered-down hair. No go.

"You didn't tell him what'd happened?"

"Of course I did. That night. Did he say anything then? No. Now, four days later—after not even bothering to drive up to see his son—he gives me grief about how I handled things? And the worst of it is, I let him get to me. Instead of just agreeing with him and ending the conversation, I argued, even though I know it never ends well. Ever."

Sighing, she inspected her hand, then got back up to pour the now-opened paint into a tray. "So that's why I'm late. Miguel, too. And he hates that, hates getting there after everybody else has already copied down their assignments for the day...."

Her voice broke. Not a lot, but enough to make Eli feel like a character in a horror movie who looks around, whispering, *"Anybody else hear that?"* a split second before Godzilla bursts through the wall.

"It wasn't your fault, Tess," Eli said quietly.

The roller soaked, Tess glanced at him, then slapped the thing against the dirty white wall. When it appeared she had no intention of answering, Eli stood, coming up behind her, wanting so badly to touch her it hurt. "I said, it wasn't your—"

"And maybe you have no idea what you're talking about," she said, her words bouncing with each jut of the roller.

"Then why don't you clue me in?"

"Because...because I don't dump on my friends, remember?"

Ah, geez...he couldn't believe she was still playing that card. Annoyed beyond belief, Eli grabbed one of her wrists anyway, making her face him, a goner for sure the moment he saw the deep, deep pain in her eyes. As if realizing her mistake, she ducked her head; Eli tucked two fingers under her chin and forced their gazes to meet again.

"So. We're friends now?"

She did this funny little shrug, like a fly had landed on her. "Maybe."

He let go, stuffing his hands in his back pockets. "Tess... when I went through some heavy personal stuff a few years ago, I didn't want to talk about it, either. Thought it was, I don't know—unmanly or something. So it's not like I don't understand where you're coming from, that you don't want people to think you're weak or whatever—"

"What kind of heavy stuff?" she said, her eyes suddenly all liquidy and soft.

"Nice try," Eli said on a dry chuckle, now folding his arms over his chest to lean back against the sink. "But this isn't about me, it's about you. And it seems to me you've got a long way to go before you're anywhere near emptied out. So get crackin', sunshine."

Shaking her head, she returned to her task, even though her hand was shaking so badly she nearly dropped the roller. "Not looking for sympathy, Eli—"

She jolted when his hand closed around her upper arm, her gaze jerking back to his. Half startled, half ticked, would be his guess.

"You know," he said softly, thinking, *Join the club,* "one day I'd like somebody to explain why being sympathetic is such a bad thing." He released her arm. "And just for the record," he added before she could interrupt, "if I had a grain of sense I *wouldn't've* followed you down the hall, wouldn't be standing here now. But I did, and I am, and the longer you put this off the more I'm thinking I might just have to kiss you. And God knows neither of us wants *that.*"

Aaaand of course, Tess's eyes immediately dropped to his mouth. If only for a moment.

*Let's hear it for sobriety, yea,* she thought, then blinked, dragging her gaze back up. Yeah, like that helped. Because every fraction deeper Eli's eyes dipped into hers, the more the final, frail thread that had barely held her together for the past year shredded. But she'd already said more, revealed more, than she'd intended....

"You're insane," she muttered, turning back to the wall.

"No, just horny. And concerned. *Really* bad combination. And you've got three seconds to start talking. One…"

"I thought we'd agreed—"

"Yeah, well, things change. Two…"

"Oh, for God's sake—give me a moment, okay?" She bent down to reload the dry roller, then shooed Eli out of her way to attack the next section of wall. His scent, his presence, swamped the small, airless space, permeating her very being and annoying the life out of her. Because clearly sobriety only went so far. As in, she had control over her actions, and even over her head. Over her body, though? Not so much.

Over the ache of being lonely and alone for far too long? Not at all.

Even so, as she muscled the poor, hapless roller, it occurred to her she could play the scenario to her own advantage, satisfying Mr. Worried Eyes while still staying in control. That sometimes, the truth is a girl's best friend.

Or at least enough of it to get her point across.

"Okay," she said at last, reloading the roller, waiting out the stab of pain before starting up again, her strokes becoming faster, shorter. Angrier. "I was in love with Enrique, Eli. Like, *seriously* in love." She glanced over; no reaction. "I thought it was mutual. And maybe it was, at the beginning. Until he decided his country needed him more than I did."

Leaning perilously close to the freshly painted wall, she shook her head. "Okay, that came out a little harsh, because I totally supported his decision to enlist after 9/11. I was scared to death for him," she said, resuming her painting, "but I was more scared of what might happen if people like Ricky *didn't* do something. But every time he came home on leave, things got…harder."

"In what way?"

"Before he left? We hardly ever argued. Suddenly we

were fighting about everything. Mostly—" the rolling picked up speed again "—about…how…I was doing things. Decisions I'd *had* to make on my own…because he wasn't *there,* or stuff I didn't feel…I should be *bothering* him about. You know, because…he had a lot more pressing things…on his *plate* than whether or not…we needed a new *couch*—"

The roller flew out of her hand; Eli caught it and tried to set it in the pan, but Tess grabbed it again, needing to keep moving. To roll away the anger, the memories.

"Enrique rarely talked about his experiences over there. Something about not wanting to 'infect us.' But I've read and heard enough…" Squatting in front of the pan to refill it, she sighed. "As hard as it was for me, dealing with the kids and everything on my own, that was a walk in the park compared with what he faced every day. So I figured it was up to me to make sure he had normal and sane and peaceful to come home to, so we could pick up where we'd left off as much as possible…"

"But…?" Eli prompted when she paused.

"But it was like somebody'd poured acid on our marriage—once the corrosion starts, there's not a whole lot you can do to stop it." She paused, breathing hard. "I knew Ricky felt like a stranger in his own house, after being away so much. Worse, though, was that we felt like strangers to each other." Turning, she said, "You want to know why the thought of Luis going over there makes me ill? Besides the obvious, I mean? Because doing that…it changes people. And not always for the better." She faced the wall again. "Every time Ricky came back, I saw less and less of the man I fell in love with, and it broke my heart. By the end, it was like we were standing on opposite sides of this big, soundproof window—we could see each other but not *hear* each other."

"Aren't there programs—?"

"We tried 'em all. Counseling, couples' retreats, you name it. Nothing worked."

"Then you did everything you could."

A half laugh preceded, "You would think, right? Except he wasn't the only one who'd changed. Because I had, too. I'd become stronger, more capable, while he was gone. Not that I had much choice. But…"

Tess doused the roller once again. "But as a sergeant, Ricky was used to being in charge. Ordering people around. Unfortunately, that didn't turn off when he came home. And after so long of being the sole decision-maker I couldn't simply be…what he wanted me to be." Her mouth flattened. "Needed me to be, I guess—the little woman who could make him feel in control of *something* in his life."

She heard Eli shift behind her. "Meaning?"

"Meaning…he found someone else."

There was a long silence, punctuated only by the rhythmic rasp of the roller against the wall. "Overseas?" Eli finally asked.

"Yeah. Some gal in the vehicle maintenance unit, apparently. It didn't last long—her tour ended before his did, and she went back to her husband in Oklahoma. He didn't tell me until he was out for good. Nor did he sound particularly remorseful."

"So you threw him out on his butt?"

"He left before I got the chance. Although, if he'd wanted to work things out, I might've still shoved my pride where the sun don't shine and tried to get past the infidelity. Give him the benefit of the doubt—you know, the stress of circumstances made him do it and all that? But Ricky all but admitted he wouldn't have cheated if it hadn't already been over between us." She felt her mouth pull into a tight smile. "He wanted out, Eli. Wanted out of our marriage a heckuva lot more than he ever wanted out of the army, since he re-upped of his own accord."

"What about the kids?"

Tess snorted. "He seemed happy enough to get me pregnant—both times—but…I don't know. Maybe if he'd been around more, he would've grown closer to them. But he wasn't, and he didn't. Still hasn't. It breaks Micky's heart."

"Not nearly as much as it breaks yours, I bet."

The wall done, her head about to explode from Eli's kindness, Tess plopped the roller into the sink to rinse it. "No, what really broke my heart was not having clue one about how to make the pieces fit. How to be what Ricky needed me to be without losing myself. All those years of trying to keep those homefires burning, only to find out I was the one fighting the losing battle. And now…" Yanking a paper towel off a nearby roll to wipe her hands, she looked at Eli, knowing her very survival depended on ignoring what she saw in his eyes. "What the kids and I have…it's not ideal, but it's working. Finally. Letting someone else into my life, their lives…" She shook her head. "I don't know how to find that balance, Eli. And I'm not sure I have the energy to try again."

After a moment, he nodded. "In a way, I can understand that."

Well, knock her over with a feather. "You…do?"

"Sure. Getting tangled up with somebody—especially when there's kids involved—you gotta ask yourself if it's worth it, you know?"

"That's it exactly," she said, even as she caught the brief shadow scuttling across his face. "I'm tired, Eli. Tired of loving people who don't love me back, tired of believing in something that doesn't seem to be in the cards for m-me—"

*Dude. What's up with the catch in the throat?*

Clearing that throat, she added, "So that's the story. Was it good for you?"

"You are too much," Eli said softly, then pushed out a

breath. "I'm sorry you had to go through that, Tess. Truly sorry. But I'm glad you told me."

"Why?"

"That's the part I haven't figured out yet," he said, straightening again. Making her jump slightly when his hand closed around hers. "I just have to say, though...not everybody who goes 'over there' comes back messed up. Some do, sure, but not all. Just like not every man cheats, no matter how much people say we're hardwired that way."

When she gave him raised eyebrows, he chuckled again. And let go. Took a sec for her nerve cells to catch on. Idiots.

"I didn't cheat on you, Tess. I never even looked at whatshername while you and I were still together. I've never two-timed *any* woman I've been with. Not my style. And some men, when they fall in love? They're more'n happy to just lay there with that one woman for the rest of their lives. Not saying you haven't had a real bad run of luck, honey," he said quietly. "But there's nothing sayin' your luck can't change. And one more thing—just because your marriage failed, that doesn't mean *you* did."

He finally, *finally* turned to leave. Only when Tess should have been breathing out a sigh of relief, she said, "Hey. Question."

Eli twisted around. "Yeah?"

"If...I hadn't opened up...*would* you have kissed me?"

Another frown preceded a long, rough sigh, which in turn led to an equally rough, sexy-as-all-hell chuckle. "I've also never forced myself on a woman. Never saw the fun in that. But I'm not above takin' advantage of an opportunity. As you well know," he added, his eyes fixed on hers. "So I guess...it would've depended."

"On what?"

One side of his mouth lifted. "Maybe you should think

about why you're even asking these questions," he said, then left, his footsteps as he tromped down the wood-floored hallway echoing in her empty brain.

## Chapter Eight

Even though Thanksgiving was right on top of them, the weather warmed up enough over the next few days so that Eli could replace the exterior trim around the windows without worrying about frostbite. Even more fortunately, Tess had been so busy with kids and new clients she'd only been able to pop in once a day to check on things, scooting back out with little more than a grateful smile and a "Looking good, guys."

Good thing, too, because whenever Eli was around her he found himself considering options not even anywhere near the table, let alone on it. Options *he'd* tabled indefinitely more than eight years ago. But man, had it been a shock to discover, when she'd told him she wasn't pregnant that he'd frankly been a mite disappointed.

Talk about a *What the hell?* moment.

He dipped a small brush into the zonk-blue paint Tess had picked out, then held the wet brush up to the cloudless sky.

Yep. Same color. Of course, he mused as he began to paint the primed wood, he supposed it wasn't all that far-fetched, him getting broody. Turning thirty did that to a person. However, even though Tierra Rosa had heard a slew of unexpected "I dos" this past little while, he imagined the Happy Ever After fairy had moved on by now.

And anyway, her kids were a deal breaker, even if she had been interested.

Even if it galled the hell out of him, the way she'd taken the lion's share of the responsibility for her marriage going bust on herself.

Even if the emptiness of his house seemed to taunt him more and more, when he'd fix himself dinner and sit at his table and find himself thinking how nice it would be to see Tess's animated face on the other side, hear her laughter. Dodge her ribbing. Maybelline did her best, but she didn't laugh much.

Nor was this the kind of loneliness assuaged by some casual hookup that'd only leave him feeling emptier afterward than before. No, this feeling of, of something *missing* went bone deep, soul deep, so deep Eli couldn't even see bottom.

But him and Tess? Pfft. Wasn't a house big enough in town to hold their combined baggage.

A truck roared up behind him; he didn't pay it any mind. These days somebody was always coming or going.

"That is some kinda blue," his brother Silas said, followed immediately by his five-year-old nephew's, "Can I help, Unca Eli?"

"I'm real sorry, sport," Eli said with a grin for Oliver, his heart melting as usual at the sight of those big brown eyes underneath English choirboy bangs. "But not this time. It's gotta go on just perfect." Eli pulled a face. "Boring. You'd hate it."

"Nuh-uh—"

"Ollie. Enough." Balancing Tad, the "baby," on his hip, Silas slammed shut the truck door and came closer, the afternoon sun glancing off the sharp nose and high cheekbones he'd gotten from their mother.

Eli grinned for the blond toddler, a year or so older than Tess's little girl, then squinted at his brother. "What brings you up here?"

"Dad said you were working miracles with this place. Decided to come see for myself." Silas knuckled back his cowboy hat, revealing spikes of dark brown hair. Through rimless glasses, he gave the spruced-up exterior an approving nod. "Looks good."

"Thanks, but it's not all me. I mean, yeah, I'm doing the work, but Tess picked everything out. The colors and stuff." Beaming, the toddler lunged for Eli, who passed the brush to his brother just in time to catch the kid. He was beginning to wonder if he *was* magnetized or something. "Heya, Tadpole, got a hug for your favorite uncle?"

"Tess?" Silas said. "Tess Montoya? The gal who chased you down Main Street with a mop?"

"It was a long time ago," Eli said as Tad gave Eli a big old hug, then smacked his sticky hands on either side of Eli's face and added a kiss for good measure. Damn.

"Tad!" Ollie called to his baby brother from the side of the house. "It's a dead squirrel! Come look!"

The squirt tried to wriggle down, only to go into a gigglefit when Eli pretended he wasn't gonna let him go. At last escaping his uncle's clutches, he went streaking off, Silas yelling at the boys not to touch the corpse, and Eli watched, conflicted, fighting all the broody feelings pecking at him like a bunch of hungry chickens. Didn't even notice his brother's hard, even more amused stare until he went to take back his brush.

"And hasn't it been a dog's age since I've seen a look like that on your face?" Silas said, grinning.

Eli jabbed the brush into the paint. "And what look would that be?"

"The got-it-bad-and-that-ain't-good look. Aw...you're blushing! Is that cute as hell or what?"

"That's sunburn."

"On your neck?" Laughing even harder, Silas dodged Eli's swipe with the wet brush. "You still got a thing for her?"

"Don't be ridiculous—"

"Unca Eli, can we go inside?"

"Sure thing, buddy." Squatting to hammer the lid back on the paint can, he darted a look at Silas. "I suppose you want to come in, too—"

"Don't try changing the subject. When did this happen? It's okay, I swear I won't tell Mom."

Eli had to laugh. "Okay, so maybe there's...something," he said as they headed toward the front door, Eli squinting into the strong, late afternoon sun rather than look at his brother. "But it's not..." Climbing the three steps to the porch, he released a breath. "It's not like anything would ever come of it, for a whole boatload of reasons."

"Such as?"

The slanting sun pierced the thick stand of pinons to the west, the day's last blast of warmth before the cold, high desert night set in. "She's not interested in a relationship and I don't date women with kids. For starters."

"Yeah, that's some real conviction I hear in your voice."

"And you can stop that train right now, Silas—"

"Why? So it doesn't run down the pea brain standing in the middle of the tracks? You're great with the boys, for pity's sake—"

"Has nothing to do with me liking kids," Eli said through

a tense jaw. "Or even getting married, having kids of my own someday." Annoyed, he streaked a hand through his hair. "Sooner rather than later, truth be told."

"Oh, yeah?"

"Yeah. I'm ready. Who knew, right? But maybe, I don't know…I'm looking for something maybe a little less ripe for potential disaster?"

"There's no guarantees, you know," Silas said quietly.

"Crap, Si…I'm sorry, that was stupid. Of course there aren't, I know that. But after—"

"You're gun-shy, I get it. No, I really do," Silas said when Eli shot him a *Yeah, right* look. "Having something blow up in your face tends to make a person not exactly eager to repeat the experience."

Pushing out a breath, Eli leaned against the porch railing. "Yeah," he said, as the trees slowly swallowed up the sun. "Bad enough when it's just the two people in the relationship and it doesn't work out. But the minute you add kids to the mix?"

He thought of Miguel's grin when Eli'd said he looked like a zombie…how badly he'd wanted to pick the little boy up and hug him, like Eli's own father had done to him a time or six when he'd been hurt or scared or sad. Like he'd done with another little boy, a long time ago. The way Julia had toddled over to him, arms lifted, trusting. How badly the kids needed a full-time dad and Eli suddenly wanted to *be* a full-time dad. And husband. But with Tess feeling the way she did…

"Too much of a risk, bro. For their sakes. So. End of discussion. You wanna see inside or what?"

The boys were chasing each other round and round the empty living room, their clear, high-pitched voices bouncing off the beamed ceiling and warm tan walls where tacky, cheap paneling had once been. Silas whistled.

"There were wood floors under that disgusting carpet?"

"Oak, no less. And look at the kitchen."

Silas peeked into the finished kitchen. "Whoa. Like night and day."

"You wanna buy it, I can probably get you a good deal."

"Thanks, but a new mortgage is the last thing I need right now. And it's too isolated." He met Eli's gaze again. "You do realize you're full of it, right?"

Eli let out a half-laugh. "You know, you've got some nerve ragging on me, considering what Mom's been doing to you. Noah told me," he added when Silas's brows lifted over his glasses. "About her efforts to fix you up with every available female in the county. I was 'supposed' to talk to Dad to get him to get Mom off your case, but—"

"It's okay, just as well you didn't. And Mom hasn't been that bad."

"Sally Perkins?"

Silas winced. "Point taken. But—"

Groaning, Eli threw his hands in the air and walked away.

"*But,*" Silas said, following him, "let me just say this—I don't know Tess all that well, other than from seeing her once a year to do her taxes or when we run into each other in town. But I like her."

"Fine. So *you* go after her."

"Nah. She's not my type."

"What the hell's that supposed to mean?" Eli said, wheeling on him.

Silas pulled up short, hands raised. Laughing. Annoyed, Eli lumbered toward the hall leading to the bedrooms, following the boys' voices.

"Not that I don't think Tess is attractive," his brother said behind him. "In fact, I'd even say she was hot."

Eli spun around again.

"You really need to get a handle on this," Silas said mildly, moments before his sons came roaring out of the back bed-room and launched themselves at his thighs. Swinging the little one up onto his hip, Silas laid a hand on Eli's shoulder. "Okay, here's a hypothetical question—let's say, just for argument's sake, I asked Tess out—"

"You wouldn't dare."

"I said it was hypothetical, numbskull. But judging from your flared nostrils right now…you might want to think about that."

Eli sighed, then crossed his arms, that ache starting up all over again as he watched Silas nuzzle Tad's soft little neck, making the baby giggle his head off. "Talk about your good intentions gone haywire," he muttered. "All I wanted was to make it up to her for what I did back then. To get back in her good graces. Had no intention of…" He pushed out a breath.

Silas looked over. "Of falling for her all over again?"

"It's not supposed to happen that way. Once something's over, it's over."

"Says who?" At Eli's rueful laugh, Silas said, "I remember how crazy you were about Tess before. And how much that scared you. So maybe this is about more than proving some-thing to Tess. It's about proving something to yourself."

"What the hell's that supposed to mean—?"

"Oooh, Unca Eli…" Stern look from the tot at three o'clock. "You cussed."

"Smarty-pants," Eli said, roaring after his laughing nephew until he caught him, grabbing him under the arms to swing him around…just as Tess appeared like a ghost in the doorway, car keys in hand, that big old bag of hers clutched under one arm.

"Oh…I wondered what was going on!" she said, looking cute as all get-out in one of her big, soft, cuddly sweaters that cut off at the waist of a pair of tight, tight, tight jeans—*thank* You, Lord!—and her lips were all glossy, her big, dark eyes rimmed with some smoky-looking stuff that made them look even bigger. "Just finished up with a client, so thought I'd drop by for a sec."

"I was just about to lock up, actually," Eli said, setting Ollie down a second before Tad accosted him, jumping up and down and chirping, "Me next! Me next!"

Tess laughed. "Boy, does that sound familiar. Hey, Silas," she said, standing on tiptoe to give his brother a quick peck on the cheek, and Eli imagined those soft, full lips on his cheek—among other places—and nearly dropped his nephew.

"Gotta pee!" Tad said, as Ollie wormed free with a "Me, too!"

"Sorry," Silas said, trundling off with his progeny in tow, "they're not exactly ready to fly solo yet…"

"Not a problem," Tess said, smiling, as they disappeared. Chuckling, she click-clicked in her high-heeled boots back toward the living room. "That's a major family activity at our house, too," she said, then yawned, covering her mouth. "Wow, sorry." She gave her head a little shake. "Front's looking good."

"Should be finished up by tomorrow."

"Mm," she said distractedly, yawning again as she crossed to a jut-out overlooking the front and sank onto the hard window seat.

"You look beat."

"Long day," she said, leaning one shoulder against the obviously cold glass to look out, the oversize purse cradled on her lap. "Not that I'm not grateful that people are at least thinking about buying houses again, but…I'm whacked."

"And you're actually admitting that?"

Tess blew a soft snort through her nose. "I also have no clue what to feed the kids tonight."

"I doubt they're expecting a gourmet meal."

"No. But they are expecting *food*. And I forgot to go shopping. No, actually, I didn't forget, I just haven't had time."

"So cut yourself some slack and pick up a pizza."

"Mm, can't. Did that yesterday. And I still have to get real food in the house."

"Before they revoke your membership in the Good Mom Club?"

"Something like that, yeah."

Listening to Silas and his boys finishing up in the bathroom, Eli walked over to inspect the new built-ins, which Teo had stained that afternoon. "I seem to recall plenty of nights my mother shoved fish sticks and Tater Tots in front of us. Or pizza. Or KFC. Sure, when she cooked, she made sure we got our veggies and whatnot, but some nights it just didn't happen. And we all survived."

"So I see," she said, then startled the hell out of him by asking, "So what's the deal, Garrett? How come you're not married?" When Eli's head whipped around, she said softly, "Eli, you look at your brother's boys the way I look at a Neiman Marcus catalog. And what you said the other day, about men who fall in love and stay fallen for the rest of their lives? Those are not the words of a confirmed bachelor. So what's up?"

He looked away, pretending to inspect a spot on one shelf, then back at her. "The timing was never right, that's all."

Still leaning into the window, Tess crossed her arms. "Why do I get the feeling there's more to it than that?" When he didn't—couldn't—say anything, she softly laughed. "Okay, unlike *some* people in this room, I'm not about to badger you into talking if you don't wanna. Waaaay too tired. But that sounding board thing? It works both ways." Then she struggled to her feet, looking around. "Tell you one thing—if the place doesn't sell, it's not because it doesn't look good."

"You worried about that?" Eli said, relieved the subject had shifted away from him.

"I'd be lying if I said I wasn't," she said on a dry laugh. "Enrique's fairly good about the child support payments, but everything else is up to me. Would be nice to see something go *into* my bank account for a change instead of only going out of it. And besides, if business doesn't pick up, we might have to let Candy go. Since it's not like she can just find another job in this town, that's not an option. But even more than that, it's…well, when I take on a client, I promise to do whatever it takes to either find them the perfect home or sell their old one. What can I say? I like making people happy."

No kidding. "Then I suppose," Eli said as he heard his brother and them come down the hall, "you've gotta trust you've done everything you can and just…let it go."

Tess blinked up at him. "Yeah, you're right. Well. This isn't getting the kids picked up and groceries bought," she said, starting toward the door. Before she got there, though, she turned, her mouth opening like she was going to say something, only the others returned before she got the chance. So all she did was mutter, "See you tomorrow," and left.

"We need to be going, too," his brother said, nodding at his youngest. "This one's about to drop. Refuses to take a nap in day care."

"Is that true?" Eli said, scooping Tad into his arms. "How you gonna grow up big like your daddy and me if you don't take your naps?"

"I don't get s'eepy," the kid said, yawning.

Still holding the little boy, Eli walked his brother and Ollie out; the sun was barely a memory, the color rapidly leaching from the sky. Silas paused, then said, "In case you think that was a private conversation back there with Tess? Wrong. She sure doesn't sound like someone with it all together."

"Oh, and like you don't sometimes feel wrung out at the end of the day? She's human, so sure life's gonna wear her down from time to time. That doesn't mean she's looking to be rescued." Eli's mouth thinned. "Since I'm sure as heck no white knight, it's all good."

"If you say so," Silas said, heading toward his truck, opening the door so Ollie could climb up into his car seat. Eli followed, too tangled up in his own thoughts to even get mad at his brother. Cupping Tad's head as the child cuddled against his chest, he again thought about how he'd been chugging along just fine all by himself, enjoying his bachelorhood, being able to do whatever he wanted, whenever he wanted, in his own house. Until here comes Tess to remind him of everything he didn't have.

And no, the irony wasn't lost on him.

"You ever get lonely?" he quietly asked as Silas reached for the dozing child.

His brother gave him a sharp look, then ducked into the backseat to buckle the little guy in. When he reemerged, he said, "Like you wouldn't believe."

"So how do you cope with it?"

A tight, wry smile stretched across Silas's lips. "I remember the pain," he said, "and that pretty much shuts the sucker up."

But after Silas drove off, Eli stood there, letting the cold seep through his work shirt and thinking...but what if that doesn't work?

Then what?

Tess raced back to the office, totally blowing off mundane things like speed limits and such. Fortunately, "rush hour" out here only meant you might actually see another vehicle in your travels, so she wasn't exactly putting others' lives—or hers—in mortal danger.

Oh, no, Eli had handily done that already.

The brakes squealed when she jerked the car up in front of the office; she got out and slammed the door so hard the whole car shuddered. Much as she had with that last, lingering look, a look that had somehow…engulfed her, threatening to simultaneously drown and buoy her. A look far, far more dangerous to her self-control than any physical contact—

"Took two messages for you," Candy said as she came out of the bathroom, rubbing lotion into her hands. "Hey—did Suze mention I'm not gonna be in the rest of the week, on account of I'm going to Kansas for Thanksgiving?"

Tess stared blankly at the woman as she wound a fluffy scarf around her neck. "Thanksgiving?"

"Yeah, you know—that holiday where we gorge on turkey and pumpkin pie? Happens every year, fourth Thursday in November?"

Silence. "And…I suppose that's this week?"

"Oh, honey…don't tell me you don't have plans?"

"Uh…sure, I just spaced it for a minute. Hey," Tess said, walking around her desk, "you have a great time with your folks."

"Oh, I'm sure I will! There's six of us, everybody with kids but me, so it's wild when we all get together. I can't wait!" she said, laughing, and disappeared into the night.

Into a life that included everything Tess had never had and thought she was getting with Enrique, only she hadn't and now here she was, facing another holiday she basically wished would simply go away.

True, as a child, Tess had always thought movies about huge families gathering for the holidays just looked…scary. Suddenly, though, the prospect of spaghetti or hot dogs or something with just her and the kids—because neither one would touch turkey, let alone pie made from a vegetable— wasn't sitting all that well.

"Stop it," she muttered, picking up the couple of messages—some clients just refused to call her cell phone on principle—as her wayward thoughts once more meandered back to The Look That Did Her In, those golden eyes crackling with a thousand conflicting impulses…impulses she understood herself all too well.

To deny she and Eli wanted each other would be stupid. And pointless. Lord, the very thought made her mouth water and her skin itch and her hoohah tingle. But it was more than that, more than just the hokeypokey she missed…she wanted…

She closed her eyes, letting go. Admitting, finally, how nice it would be to let someone else do the heavy lifting for a change, damn it. Not forever, not all the time, but just…every now and then—

"What's up with you?" Suze said, startling her.

"Geez, where'd you come from?"

"Just got in. Shopping," she said, hefting a Macy's bag. "Getting a jump on Christmas. The Albuquerque traffic sucks, though. I remember when you could get between any two points in the city in fifteen minutes or less. No more. Of course, that was twenty years ago. So…everything okay?" she prodded as Tess decided it wouldn't be politic to mention that twenty years ago, she'd been a fifth grader.

"Sure," Tess said brightly, getting a glimpse of black suede and cashmere as she pinned the messages up on her cork board. "Just busy, lost in my own world."

Leaning one skinny hip on the front of Tess's desk, Suze crossed her arms, swinging a foot shod in something spiky and expensive. "How's the Coyote Trail place coming along?"

"Nearly done. First open house is…wow. This Saturday."

"Well, good luck to you. I mean, God knows the agency could use the commission, but I'm not holding my breath."

"Gee, Suze—"

"Oh, don't take it personally. But in this market—"

"Some people are still buying houses, amazingly enough. And even if it doesn't sell, the Harrises can use it as a rental."

"Not the same as a sale, though."

"True," Tess said on a sigh. "So we just have to think positive, right? Eli says we just have to know we've done everything we can and trust the outcome."

Tess wondered if Suze had any idea how crinkly the skin around her eyes got when she narrowed them like that. "Just a warning, girlfriend," she said, sliding off the desk. "The man is an insatiable flirt. But he's not real good at following through, if you know what I mean."

Took a second before Tess's poor pooped brain sorted out the roughly half dozen inferences in those few sentences. Sliding right on past the more obvious ones, she said, "You went out with Eli?" And no, she didn't even try to hide her incredulity. Imagining Mr. Laid Back with Miss Prissypants was so not working.

"Ages ago," Suze said with a flick of her wrist. "Thought I had a halfway decent chance, too, since I don't have kids. You do know he categorically refuses to get involved with single mothers, right?"

"So I gathered."

When Tess volunteered nothing more, it seemed to take Suze a second or two to regroup. "Every other woman who crosses his path, though," she said, back on track," is fair game. You might want to keep that in mind."

Not that this was news—on either count—but what was with the ridiculous, acid-reflux-esque spurt of jealousy? One quickly tamped when the logical side of Tess's brain piped up and reminded her the man could flirt—and do anything else, to be honest—with whoever he damn well chose. Since, you know, nobody had any claim on anybody else, the occasion-ally shared, longing glance notwithstanding. Not to mention one memorable night's shenanigans.

To mention such things, however, would be mean. Not to mention tacky as hell.

"Nothin' goin' on, Suze," she whispered, hiking her purse back onto her shoulder, "but thanks for the tip. Well, I'm outta here—kids to fetch, dinner to hunt down."

"Lord, better you than me, is all I gotta say," Suze said as she sashayed back to her desk. "How you manage all by yourself is beyond me."

Tess opened her mouth, only to think, *Why?*

Minutes later, the kids once more under her jurisdiction, she pulled up in front of Garcia's Supermarket, set off by itself out on the highway leading to town. Housed in what used to be somebody's stuccoed, territorial-style ranch house, what the store lacked in selection or slickness it more than made up for in convenience.

And right now, Tess was all about convenience.

Her first-grader, however, was all about Thanksgiving, mutant construction-paper turkeys and all. "Miss Albright says," he went on from his booster seat behind her, "it's when families get together and say what they're grateful for. Do you know what grateful means?"

"Uh-huh," Tess said wearily, hauling the baby out of her seat as Micky unlatched his own belt. "Do you?"

"It's when you're glad about stuff." Falling into step beside Tess as she carted the heavy, sleepy baby into the store, he added, "Miss Albright told us to make a list of all the stuff we were grateful for. Wanna hear?"

"Um…sure, sweetie." She yanked free an ancient, wobbly grocery cart from the herd stuffed helter-skelter just inside the front door and lowered Julia into it, strapping her in. Kid let out a screech and lunged toward a display of crackers; in a single, practiced move, Tess grabbed a box of Ritz, ripped it open and handed one to her daughter. *Please, God, let there be a chicken. Or at least a bag of nuggets—*

"I'm grateful for you, and Julia, and Aunt Flo—"

Score! Two of the suckers lay on a bed of ice in the cooler case.

"Hey, Miss Teresa," Little Jose—in his fifties, at least, his father Big Jose yelling in Spanish to somebody on the phone in the back—said with a wide grin. Which, unfortunately, didn't detract all that much from the smears of animal blood on his apron. "You want one of these beauties?"

"—and Winnie and Aidan and Thea and all her dogs and—"

"Both, actually. And would you mind cutting one of them into pieces? It'll cook quicker that way."

"Sure, no problem," Jose said, pulling the pallid birds from their chilly bed.

"—an' all my friends at school, and Eli."

*Thwack!* went the cleaver. Out of sight, thank God—

"Eli?"

"Uh-huh."

Tess laughed. "You barely know him—how on earth did Eli make your list?"

"'Cause he said I looked like a zombie."

Of course.

*Thwack! Thwack!*

"—an' Miss Albright said putting people on our list means we're thinking good thoughts about them, which makes them feel good even if they don't know we're thinking about them. So are we having lots of people over for Thanksgiving? And a big turkey an' stuff?"

Nodding her thanks to Jose when he handed her the chickens, all snug in their white butcher paper cocoons, Tess steered the cart toward the refrigerator cases for milk and juice. "You don't like turkey, remember?"

"Then I'll just have the pumpkin pie." He started skipping beside her. "Are you gonna make it or buy it?"

She was so gonna kill this teacher.

"Honey…not everybody has a big Thanksgiving. Some people like to be alone. Or some smaller families just celebrate with each other." She paused. "Like us."

"No party?"

Tess frowned down at him. "Honey…we've never made a big deal about the holidays before. Why are you so hot about this now?"

"'Cause it sounds like fun."

"Well, we can make our own fun, right? Just you and me and Julia?"

Oh, God…spare her the puppy-dog eyes.

"Tell you what…" Spying a can of pumpkin pie mix, Tess grabbed it and tossed it into her cart, hoping if God had seen fit to send her chickens, He'd also provide a frozen pie shell. Her eyes on her rapidly deflating son, she turned into what must have been the dining room in the original house, now lined with freezer cases. Thea had once lived in a converted convenience store; this was a house turned into a store. Ditch your preconceived notions, all ye who enter Tierra Rosa. Tess smiled for her little boy. "We can have your favorite thing for dinner, how's that? Whatever you like— Omigosh!" she said when her cart rammed into someone else's. "I'm so sorry—!"

"Teresa?" Donna Garrett said. "What a hoot to run into you here! Literally!" Clogs clomped on the bare wood floor as Eli's mother scooted around her own cart to pull Tess into a long, steady hug. "How are you, honey?"

"Um, fine?" Tess mumbled into an ancient, slightly musty-smelling Peruvian poncho, only to find herself jerked back a second later, as, her hands on Tess's shoulders, Eli's mother backed up to take stock with warm brown eyes as sharp as her faded red hair—loosely caught up with assorted clips around her pretty, unlined face. "I can't tell you how often I think about you. Especially this last little while."

The unexpected encounter, as well as Donna's effusive and unfeigned warmth, clogged Tess's throat. She'd always liked Eli's mother, but more than that nobody knew how much she'd found the Garretts' crazy, noisy house a refuge from the stony silence of her own. How much, in a way, she'd been almost angrier with Eli for ripping that away than himself. "I think about you, too," she said, smiling.

Smiling, Donna briefly cupped Tess's cheek before glancing at the baby, who was staring at her, transfixed. "Oh, my goodness…isn't she gorgeous! What's her name?"

"Julia."

"The Spanish pronunciation, how pretty. How old?"

"Two last month."

"You're kidding! Honestly, I lost a year in there somewhere…which makes this little guy…?"

"Six," Micky said.

"Unbelievable." Donna reached into the freezer case for a package of frozen peas. "You all ready for Thanksgiving?"

"Mama said we can have anything I like," Miguel put in, "since I hate turkey and nobody's comin' over."

"Micky, honestly—"

Donna gave her a startled look. "You're *not* spending Thanksgiving alone?"

"Sweetie—would you please get a carton of orange juice out of the case over there?"

"The one with the duck on it?"

Tess gave him a thumbs-up, then turned back to Donna. "Mom and her husband are going on a cruise," she said mildly.

"And my aunt's been invited to go with Winnie and Aidan to New York for the weekend. Aidan's having his first show at a New York gallery. It's opening the night after Thanksgiving. It seems everyone's either going out of town or have family coming in, so…yeah, we're just having a quiet day. I, um, thought we could get out the tree, start decorating it…"

Miguel trooped back with the juice, carefully hefting it into the cart. Donna watched him for a moment before lifting bright eyes to Tess. "Why don't you and the children come to our house for dinner?"

"Um, I don't think—"

"Oh, I know you and Eli didn't part on the most amicable of terms, but for heaven's sake, honey—that was in high school. And besides, I gather you're getting along okay now, working together on that house and everything—"

"Is there gonna be pumpkin pie?" Miguel asked.

"Oh my Lord, yes. With *lots* of whipped cream."

At the mention of whipped cream, her sugar baby looked up at her, pleading. Not that Tess couldn't wield a can of Reddi-wip as well as the next person, but…

She looked down into that eager, hopeful face, waited out the twinge, then turned back to Donna. "I don't know. It could be…awkward." *Although not for the reason you think.*

"Only if you let it be," Donna said gently, smiling for Julia, face plastered with crumbs as she boogied to the music from the Spanish-language station on the radio. "And don't you want to make the holiday more festive for their sakes?"

Festive. Right. Not high on her list. Even before things had gone sour between her and Enrique, he'd been home so seldom, and making a fuss even then had always seemed so…forced.

"I just don't want to impose," she said, and Donna laughed again.

"Spoken like somebody who's never been to a Garrett

Thanksgiving. Teresa, sweetheart, I'm serious—nothing would make me happier than to have you join us. If nothing else, to balance out all that testosterone!"

Finally, Tess nodded. "Okay, fine," she said, and Micky let out a whoop of joy, then wiggled his skinny little butt in a bizarre victory dance. Donna clapped her hands together and burst out laughing; Tess smiled. "What can I bring?"

"Just yourselves, honey," Donna said, leaning over to give Tess a quick hug. "See you around four, then?"

"Four. Got it."

As the older woman steered her cart away, Micky said, "Guess we've got something else to be grateful for, huh?"

Not exactly the word Tess had in mind.

## Chapter Nine

"What do you mean, you invited Tess and the kids to Thanksgiving?" Phone clamped to his ear, Eli stopped stirring the bubbling pot of chili as Belly writhed around his ankles, being a nuisance. Cat had a real thing for chili. Except for the beans.

"It was the Christian thing to do," his mother said, and Eli groaned, once again wondering how his mother could seamlessly blend her heartfelt faith with her hippie roots. "And you can stop that groaning right now. We ran into each other at Garcia's and I asked her what she was doing for the holiday, just making small talk, and she mentioned as how she and the children would be all by themselves and that just wasn't right, Elijah. That precious little boy, especially—you should've seen his sweet little face light up. I can only imagine how rough it's been on him, hardly ever seeing his daddy. And it can't be easy on Tess, being on her own so much. Elijah? You still there?"

He tossed a chunk of chilified hamburger at the cat, who scarfed it down, purring, then sat up like a prairie dog, begging for more. "This wouldn't be you trying to fix me up, would it?"

"Now what on earth put that idea into your head? Of course not. Since when have I ever interfered in you boys' lives?"

And yes, she was dead serious. "Sorry," Eli said. "Just checking. So. Thanks for the heads-up."

"Well, I didn't want to spring it on you, then have you go acting all weird and whatnot. And wear something nice, for heaven's sake, instead of coming here looking like you just worked for three days straight."

"Mom—"

But she was gone.

Feeling like fireworks were exploding inside his skull, Eli slopped chili into a large bowl for himself and a small one for the cat—hold the onions—then placed both on the table and dropped into his chair. Belly heaved her fat self up onto the table, gave him a questioning *Mrrrk?* and started chowing down. Eli, however, sagged back in his chair, poking his spoon in the lumpy concoction and feeling like some outside force was shoving him around his own life. And no, he didn't mean his when-have-I-ever-interfered? mother, although she wasn't helping matters.

For a moment he watched the cat, happily inhaling her snack—stoking up for the next six-hour nap—almost envying her simple, unfettered life. Except he wasn't a cat and sleeping twenty hours out of twenty-four had never been a life goal. Except maybe when he was fifteen. What he was, was a thirty-year-old man who needed to take back his life. Or at least make a concerted effort to stop letting his hormones lead him around by the nose.

He released a dry laugh. And there was the crux of it,

wasn't it? That it wasn't his mother annoying him, it was his own mixed up feelings about Tess, and her kids, and how what he was feeling more strongly every day made no sense, given the impossibility of the situation. That here he'd been counting his blessings that the job was nearly over and they wouldn't have to see each other every day because, frankly, he wasn't sure how much longer he was gonna be able to keep up the pretense of…whatever it was he was pretending.

Not that he'd skip Thanksgiving, tempting as it was. Last thing he wanted was to hurt his mother's feelings on her favorite day of the year. Or do anything that would get tongues to wagging.

"So," he said to the cat, now cleaning her whiskers in front of him, "guess all I can do is suck it up and go. And stay out of Tess's way." The cat stopped, tongue sticking out, looking at him slightly cross-eyed, as if to say, *Who?* "The little brunette who was here the other night?"

The cat reared back, her ears flat, then shot off the table.

Eli had no idea what to make of that, but something told him it wasn't good.

Like it wasn't crazy enough when the regular family was all together. Add in both of Eli's grandmothers, three of their friends from the retirement home, some chick Noah had started dating, like, five minutes ago and a few random people from church Eli didn't even know and insanity didn't even come close to describing it.

And his mother was in seventh heaven.

"Eli!" she yelled from the living room, where she stood counting the folding chairs already set up along the white tableclothed, end-to-end banquet tables, all borrowed from church. "Bring in three more chairs from the garage, your father didn't set enough."

"What are you talking about?" Dad said. "There's us, the grandmas, and the extras…that comes to sixteen, right?"

"I might have asked a couple more people," his mother mumbled, trundling into the kitchen as Dad yelled after her, "Why don't you just invite the whole damn town to begin with, save some of us the wear and tear on our nerves?"

"Wasn't me invited the Larsons," Mama yelled right back. "Or that poor Mr. Wright, bless his heart…"

Chuckling despite an almost suffocating trepidation, Eli retrieved the three chairs and carted them to the living room—the dining room not being nearly large enough to accommodate the masses—wedging them alongside their companions as Mama scurried back out with two baskets of rolls, the last-minute panic attack having officially settled in. Her heart was in the right place, but her nerves weren't exactly there with it. Or her hair, huge pieces of it floating around her flushed face.

"Damn, Mom—you seriously need to chill."

"Don't tell your mother to chill!" she said, swatting him with a potholder. "And don't swear on Thanksgiving! Oh! Somebody get the door!"

Might as well be him. Eli crossed to the front door and swung it open to the gaggle of strangers standing on their porch, all brimming with holiday cheer despite a thick layer of clouds that had brought on an early dusk. A light snow had begun to fall, the flakes glittering in the beams from the street-lamps and security lamp on the guy's garage across the street. No Tess, he noted, as anxious as his mother as he let them all in. Then he saw her SUV pull in behind the last car parked on the street, and his heart started whispering that everything he'd told his mother—and himself—had been for naught.

He watched as Tess and the kids scooted down the street, then up the walk, the snow frosting three dark heads. Miguel clutched a small bouquet of supermarket flowers; Tess was carting something in a Target bag. At the bottom of the porch steps, she glanced up, saw him, and looked—he was guessing—ready to turn right back around.

"Let me guess. Your mother didn't tell you we were coming."

"Oh, no. She did—"

"How come you're mad, Eli?"

Embarrassment slicing through him, Eli smiled for the boy, aching to brush the snow off those soft curls. "Where'd you get that idea?"

"Your constipated expression?" Tess said sweetly.

Sighing, Eli stood aside to let them in, the scent of Tess's shampoo or skin stuff or whatever it was cutting straight through the roast turkey and woodsmoke smells saturating the house.

"Miguel!" Eli's mother yelled over the roar of conversation and laughter. "You made it! Come see all the pies, sweetie…."

"Will I ever see him again?" Tess asked, first handing Julia, then the bag, to Eli so she could shuck off her knee-length sweater, which Granny Garrett whisked away, beatific smile affixed to her wrinkled face.

"Um…thank you!" Tess called after her, then took her daughter back, brows raised.

"Mom assigns both grandmas a task to keep them out of trouble," he said. "GG's is cloakroom duty." They stood there, gazes locked for way too long, until Eli finally said, "Think we can get through this like grown-ups?"

"I'm game if you are."

*Okay. On the count of three…two…one…* Smiling, he lifted the bag. "What's in here?"

"Biscochitos. I don't usually make them this early, but I had all the ingredients so I thought, what the heck. My grandmother's recipe. Hard-core traditional."

"You made these yourself?"

"With my own widdle hands, yep. Hey, they're not for you—"

But he'd already filched one of the Mexican sugar cookies from the bag and bitten into it, savoring the spicy blend of cinnamon and anise. "God, those are good."

And God, he loved the way her eyes lit up. "Not everybody likes them."

"No accounting for the idiots of the world," he said, this time getting a smile. Emboldened, he took another cookie. "I could happily live off these the rest of my life."

"Which would be short since they're made with lard. A health nut, Abuela Essie was not. Which might account for her checking out when I was four." The baby propped on her hip, she snatched the bag from his hands. "Geez, leave *some* for everybody else. Here, keep an eye on the baby while I go see if your mom needs any help."

With that, she plopped her mini-me into his arms and vanished into the crowd, leaving Eli frowning after her.

Missing her.

Hell.

Then he looked down into a pair of dark, guileless eyes designed to make people fall in love with her, and the baby grinned at him, yawned and snuggled into his sweatshirt with her thumb in her mouth…and Eli's heart shuddered and sighed and just plain gave up the good fight.

Things weren't exactly going according to plan. At all.


"Oh, no, honey—I don't need any help, everything's under control…"

Tess forcibly wrenched the potato masher out of Donna's hands, then carted the Dutch oven filled with crumbling boiled potato slices over to the counter, shoving aside an untold number of dirty bowls and pans and empty cans and open sugar bags and a hundred other victims of the woman's generous soul to set it down. In the center of the kitchen table sat a magnificently browned turkey the size of Wisconsin, surrounded by at least six pies and a dozen casseroles of green beans and stuffing and corn and what looked like at least three different sweet potato dishes.

"I can do this while you make the gravy," she said to the obviously frazzled woman, her hair reminding Tess of the tail feathers on Micky's paper turkeys.

"Now, honey, you're a guest—"

"Donna? From one control freak to another—you're never gonna win this battle. So you may as well give up now and save yourself the breath."

After a moment, Eli's mother laughed, then dumped a cup of flour into the turkey pan and took a whisk to it. "No matter how early a start I get, the last twenty minutes always turn me into a basket case. And I've never had anybody able or willing to help before—the boys are useless, the lot of 'em—so... thank you."

Tess grabbed a carton of milk from the fridge, poured some into the potatoes. "My pleasure."

The women worked in silence together for a few minutes, Tess mashing and Donna stirring, until Tess pronounced the fluffy, buttery potatoes done and started in on clearing some of the debris from the counter.

"Oh, no, just let that sit...it'll all wait until after dinner—"

"Yeah, that's the thing about dirty dishes," Tess said, sticking a gunked-up pot under the hot running water. "They don't escape out the back door while you're eating. Think how much better you're gonna feel when you come back in later and see most of this done—"

She squawked when the older woman clamped her hands around her shoulders and steered her away from the sink and back toward the living room. "You're an angel, but I didn't invite you here to play scullery maid. Now get your cute little self out there and mingle. Silas?" she called out when she opened the door. "You mind taking Teresa off my hands? She wandered in here and can't seem to find her way out again." When Eli's grinning older brother came near, a little boy attached to each long leg, Donna said in a stage whisper, "I think she's shy."

Tess squawked again, but Donna had already vanished back down her rabbit hole. Then it hit Tess which brother she'd been foisted on.

"Oh, God, Silas," she said, as Miguel appeared, commandeered both little boys and disappeared again into the crowd. "I'm so sorry—"

"S'okay, throwing women in my direction is what Mom does. At least you're a lot prettier than most of 'em," he said with a wink. Briefly touching her elbow, he nodded toward an old-fashioned buffet loaded with soft drinks. "Want something to drink?" He leaned over and said in a low voice, "There's beer out in the garage, but on account of the church folk we kinda keep it under wraps."

Tess laughed, admitting to herself that between the company, the food smells and the warmth she was feeling almost mellow. "Hit me up with the orange stuff. I haven't had that in years."

Silas dumped ice into a plastic cup, the drink fizzing and foaming when he poured it in. "You keepin' your distance from my brother?" he said as she took her first sip, sending bubbles up her nose.

After coughing for several seconds, she gave him a sharp, if watery-eyed, look. "That obvious, huh?" she choked out.

"Uh, yeah."

"Where is he anyway?" she asked, scanning the throng.

"Do you care?"

"Only because he has one of my kids."

"Over there," Silas said, gesturing with his can of Dr Pepper to the back corner of the room, where Eli sat on the sofa in a shadowed corner, Julia totally sacked out in his arms and his expression awestruck. Tess froze, squeezing the flimsy cup so hard the ice rattled. "As you can see," Silas said softly, "she's in very capable hands."

"I don't get it, Si. He's obviously great with kids—"

"Crazy about 'em."

"So why—?"

"You'd have to ask him that," Silas said as his mother hauled in Big Bird from the kitchen, a bright smile lighting up her flushed face.

"Let's eat!" she said, clunking the bird onto the table amid assorted "About damn time!" and "Oh, my—you outdid yourself this time, Donna!" and "What did she say?" from at least two of the old ladies.

"Is there somewhere Julia can sleep while we eat?" Tess asked, eyeing the throng swarming the table like locusts on the last ear of corn.

"Back bedroom. Mom keeps toddler beds and a crib in there for the grandkids. Should I save you a seat?"

"Yes, please," she said, feeling like a salmon fighting its way upstream as she squeezed through the masses toward Eli and her sleeping child.

"Hate to disturb the two of you," she said, bending over her baby, "but trust me, we'll all be happier if I put her down during dinner."

"I can—"

"You don't know the secret move," she said, scooping the unconscious child into her arms.

"I'll save you a place then?"

"Not necessary, I'm sitting next to Silas," she said, then started down the hall....

...Eli's gaze boring into her back the whole way.

"Okay, Mr. Grumpy Gus," Eli's mother said when, some time later, Eli unceremoniously dumped the platter with the decimated turkey carcass on the kitchen table. "What's up? You glowered all the way through dinner."

"Did not," he said, annoyed as all hell.

"Did, too. And if my guess is correct," she said, setting a stack of dessert plates on the table, "Tess sittin' beside Silas had something to do with that."

"That's nuts," he said, and his mother laughed, and Eli ripped off the lone wing and jabbed it in his mother's direction, only to decide he didn't want it anyway. "Call me crazy," he said, wiping his hands on a paper towel, "but I thought you invited Tess to fix her up with *me.*"

"I didn't invite her to fix her up with *anybody,*" Donna said, spooning coffee into the supersize maker, also borrowed from church, adding, "And don't you go snorting at me, young man," when Eli snorted. "You made it perfectly clear you weren't interested. I do listen, you know."

Eli tried to hold in the laugh, he really did. Didn't work.

"Lord," Donna said, lifting her eyes to heaven, "what did I do to get such children?"

"What did we do to get such a mother?" he said, giving her a hug and grabbing the can of whipped cream, shaking it and squirting it directly into his mouth.

"Give me that, for heaven's sake—anyway," she said, setting the can out of his reach, "then Tess came in and started helping me in the kitchen, and Silas was just sort of there, and you wrote yourself out of the script, so I might've...taken advantage of the opportunity. She's a lovely young woman, Eli," she said when he glowered. "I'd be pleased as punch to have her in the family."

"Doesn't matter which brother she marries, as long as one of us does. Is that it?"

"Honey, the way she attacked these pots and pans?" she said, jamming them—now clean—back into a lower cabinet with much crashing and rattling, "I wouldn't mind if your *father* married her."

"You might have a better chance with him than either one of us."

"That's what worries me," she said, straightening, face glowing and hair wild. "No, I take that back, what worries me is you sittin' there, looking like you just drank bleach because Tess is sitting with your brother, instead of doing something about it."

"Like what?"

"Pulling your head out of your butt would be a good place to start. And don't you dare walk outta here without taking those dessert plates with you!"

Halfway to the door, Eli turned, grabbed the stack of plates and stormed out, practically chucking them at the buffet—now lined with pies—before continuing on outside, not even caring how cold it was.

Except Tess had beat him to it, standing on the front porch and looking up at the stars that'd come out after the piddly snow, all wrapped up in one of the half-dozen fleece throws that graced the living-room furniture.

He could feel her loneliness from ten feet away.

Or maybe that was his.

Tess had actually made it all the way through dinner before succumbing to goodwill overload, from having years of shattered dreams shoved in her face, however unwittingly.

Mocked, that's what she felt—not by anyone inside the house, certainly, but by life or fate or whatever you wanted to call it. How nice it would've been, she thought on a harsh sigh, to simply enjoy the evening without envy's nasty little tentacles wrapping themselves around her neck.

The porch floorboards creaked behind her; she jerked around in time to hear a deep, annoyed, "You trying to freeze to death or what?"

She snuggled farther into the fabric's soft, deep pile. "This thing is amazingly warm, actually." As was Eli's voice. And his body heat when he came closer. Drat.

"Baby still asleep?"

"Out like a light. One of your grandmothers is with her. Not the cloakroom attendant, the other one." She smiled. "Something tells me the old girl would fend off a grizzly bear to protect the baby."

"You'd be right. And Miguel?"

"With Silas's boys. They adore him. And he loves having them look up to him. I haven't seen him that happy in…a long time." She glanced in his direction, but this far from that obnoxious porch light, the dark cloaked his features. "I had a great time tonight, too," she said, because she really had, the nasty tentacles notwithstanding. "I'm really glad I came."

"So I gathered."

Tess frowned. "Is something wrong?"

"No!" Then Eli released a mighty sigh. "Except me acting like a cranky toddler."

"I don't understand."

"Good—"

"Oh, no," she whispered, realizing. "You're *not* ticked because I sat next to your brother?"

"Don't be ridiculous, of course not—"

"You are! I'm really good at reading body language and—"

"You're really good at everything, aren't you?" But before Tess could even sort out the rudeness from the obvious hurt—a hurt that she suspected went way deeper than some imagined jealousy over his brother's being her dinner companion—Eli gave his head a hard shake, backing toward the door. "You know, I should retreat now before I make any more of an ass of myself—"

"No, don't," Tess said, grabbing his hand, just to keep him from leaving—God knew why—only when she let go Eli grabbed hers back, then tugged her to him, his gaze touching hers for about half a second—barely long enough for a *Wha*—? to skate through her brain—and lowered his mouth to hers.

She tensed, startled, then thought, *What the hell?* and kissed him back, no grappling involved, no body parts touching except lips, the merest suggestion of tongue, their linked hands…and Eli's strong, rough fingers on the nape of her neck. Whee, *doggie,* she kissed him back, and he kissed her back more, and basically she turned into one big quivering mass of goo.

Just from his lips touching hers? Holy cow.

When it was over—much too soon—Eli chuckled again, sheepish, and Tess had to grab the railing, she was quivering so badly.

"This isn't working, is it?" he said, and Tess barked out a laugh.

"Our staying out of each other's way? No. Apparently not."

"And I just made an ass of myself again, didn't I?"

"Didn't exactly fend you off, did I?"

"It was the moment, right?"

What is this, twenty questions? she thought, then said, lightly, "Life's made up of moments," before turning away from him, from the confusion and frustration in his eyes.

From her own, boiling up inside her like lava. She hesitated, then said, "And I probably shouldn't say this…but that was one of the nicer ones."

"Yeah?"

"Oh, yeah." Tess felt a wry smile stretch across her cold cheeks. There hadn't been a whole lot of kissing that night at his place—not lips on lips, anyway—because that would've been too intimate. Too personal. Too real. She blew out a sigh. "But just for your information—" *and to smartly tiptoe out of this minefield* "—I'm not good at everything. I'm used to making all the major decisions impacting my life and my kids', yes, but there's a lot of stuff I totally suck at."

He crossed his arms. "Like what?"

Her laugh came out sorta shaky. "After three years I still can't figure out my damn cable remote. And I can't bake a cake worth a damn. Or climb a ladder without getting dizzy. And I let your brother do my taxes because I'm petrified of making a mistake and bringing the wrath of the IRS down on my head. So, see? Not perfect."

"You kill your own bugs?"

Another laugh bubbled out. "Actually I do the catch-and-release thing. Although there's been this spider living up near the ceiling in my kitchen for months." She shrugged. "Like a bug zapper without that annoying *zzzzzzt* every five seconds."

Eli watched her for a moment, his mouth working, before touching her arm. "Come on, I got something to show you."

"What? Where?" she said as he started down the steps. "Wait—I can't just leave the kids without telling somebody where I am—"

"Meet me at the shop in five," he said, then paused. "Although if you don't, I'll completely understand."

Several beats passed as she watched him, weighing her

options. Having no idea what the consequences were to any of them. What the kiss had meant, what going with him now would mean. Something told her he had no clue, either.

"I'll be there," she said, then hurried inside to check on her kids to make sure they were happy and safe.

Her own safety, however, was another issue entirely.

Eli had no idea what he was doing.

*Yeah, like that was news,* he thought as he unlocked the shop's front door, the fluorescent lights buzzing to life when he hit the switch. Why on earth he'd kissed Tess, why he'd asked her to come here, now, since she'd see the table at the house tomorrow anyway... Definitely not the actions of a sane, rational man.

Uh, yeah. What had all that been about regaining control of his life—?

"Knock, knock."

He turned, drinking her in. Realizing he'd lost the battle...and that surrender had never felt so good.

She'd ditched the throw and was back in her megasweater, but she crossed her arms over her ribs, shivering. "Why does it feel colder in here than outside?"

"Don't know," Eli said, flicking on a space heater in the corner; it immediately glowed red, like a monster irritated at having been disturbed. "It's always been like that. Hotter'n hell in the summer, too—"

"Is that what you wanted to show me?" Tess breathed, staring at the plank table in the middle of the room.

"Yeah. Like it?"

"Like it? Oh, Eli...it's incredible." Still hugging herself, she moved closer, reaching out, then pulling back her hand. "Can I touch it?"

"Sure. The varnish should be dry by now."

Her lips curved, she ran her fingers over the worn, pock-marked surface. "This is freaking amazing," she said, her voice hushed. "It looks like something Coronado brought with him. I can practically see a bunch of conquistadores seated around it." She laughed. "And the toothless, bosomy old crone serving them."

"That was the idea," he said, ridiculously pleased. "The wood's all recycled. I just beat it up a bit for that been-around-for-a-while look."

"But…" Shaking her head, she faced him. "It's so much more than I expected. That's a lot of effort to put into something with no guarantee of return."

"And maybe not everything's about what you get back," he said softly, coming up beside her to lean his palms against the table's edge. "More often than not, there's just as much satisfaction in the doing. In…enjoying the moment."

"You're just full of surprises, aren't you?"

Chuckling, Eli walked to the end of the table, bending over to make sure the edge was evenly stained. "I like making the pieces fit," he said, straightening, his eyes steady in hers. "Turning nothin' into something. Not saying I don't enjoy the end result, but I get just as much pleasure out of the process."

"But your costs…don't you have to at least think about making a profit?"

Now he laughed out loud. "I told you, most of this is recycled. Even the hardware, what there is of it. So my out-of-pocket costs are pretty minimal. What can I tell you? I'm not one for tossin' something in the garbage just because it's a little dinged around the edges. You try hard enough, look at something with new eyes, nine times out of ten you can see ways to make it work again. To give it a second chance." He grinned. "Just like…you're doing with the house, right?"

"Of course. Right." She shoved her hair behind one ear. "Well. This really will look fantastic in the house. But, um, I suppose I should be getting back—"

"Not yet. The table's..." *No turning back now, buddy...* "That's not why I asked you to come out here."

Her eyes cut to his. "Oh?"

Eli nodded toward one of the benches. "You may as well sit, this might take a while." When she did—frowning—he leaned back against the table, clutching the edge on either side of his hips. Hard. "Gossip's kinda like a mongrel dog, you know? Mutt's still recognizable as a dog, but it's not always easy to tell what its parents or parents' parents were. Yeah, I was an idiot back in high school. And it's true I've messed around with a few women since then, but...well, you don't know the whole story. And neither do all the busybodies congratulatin' you on gettin' out while the gettin' was good."

She frowned. "If I don't know the whole story, Eli, it's not because I didn't want to hear it."

"I know that. Just like I know I've been a hypocrite, goading you into being open with me about your past when I haven't exactly returned the favor. Especially since I hated having you believe the half-truths. And yet, in another way it was almost easier to let you think the worst of me than to give you all the facts. At least at first."

"Why?" she said, caution darkening her eyes.

Eli glanced away, then back, a not-quite-smile on his lips. "To save my own sorry hide, why do you think?"

"I'm sorry, I don't—"

"Her name was Keri," he said softly. "And I loved her with everything I had in me." He paused, waiting for his heart to uncramp. "Almost as much as I loved her little boy."

## Chapter Ten

Tess caught her breath: It was like watching someone age ten years in as many seconds. Not that she hadn't jettisoned the notion of Eli's chronic adolescence some weeks ago—big difference between child*like* and child*ish*—but clearly he was about to revisit a part of his past that had clearly taken a toll in ways he never let most of the world see. That he was about to let her see him at his most vulnerable was gratifying…if unnerving. Then her heart fisted. Oh, dear God…

"When was this?"

"Shortly after you and Enrique left town. I was twenty-one, twenty-two—she was a few years older. A single mom. Justin…" Tess saw him swallow. "He was four. Cutest kid you ever saw. Probably still is," he said, and he lungs released that breath. *Okay. Not dead.* Except whatever had happened had clearly left Eli in just as much pain.

"This was here?"

"No. Dad got a contract up in Taos. Big ski resort. Keri worked in the office. She…" He punched out a breath. "I knew I was in over my head, that she needed more than I could probably offer, but she was also the first person to treat me like a grown-up. I *felt* like a grown-up when I was with her. And Justin. She told me his dad had walked out on her and the boy, that she hadn't heard from him in months. Said they'd never been married he didn't feel any obligation to stick around. So I guess it felt pretty good, having somebody need me like she did. The kid, too."

The beginnings of anger on his behalf began to prickle. "Did you help her financially?"

"No," Eli said with a vehement head shake. "It was nothing like that. I mean, sure, I took 'em out to eat every now and again, gave 'em both little presents from time to time, but she never asked for anything. I wouldn't've had it to give her anyway. Not then. The point is, though, for the second time in my life, I fell. And fell hard. For both of them. Only this time, I thought I could handle it. Thought I was ready to be a husband and father. The way the kid's eyes would light up when he'd see me…well. You know what that feels like."

Her eyes burning, all Tess could do was nod.

A smile flickered around Eli's mouth before he stood, walking over to the heater to warm his hands. "One Friday after we'd been together for about a year, I went up there after work, like I always did. Only when I got to her house, her car wasn't there. Her neighbor came outside, saying some man had shown up the day before when Keri wasn't there, said he was her husband come to take her back."

"Her husband? So she'd—"

"Lied, yeah. She called, maybe a week later, all apologetic that she hadn't been up-front with me, hoped I could find it in my heart to forgive her someday. Turns out she and this husband of hers had actually been talking on the phone for weeks, but she hadn't said anything because she honestly hadn't believed anything would come of it. When I asked her how she could go back to someone who'd walked out on her, you know what she said? 'He's Justin's father, what else can I do?'" Eli let out a dry laugh. "For more than a year, *I'd* been that little boy's father in every way that counted. And suddenly…" He shook his head.

Tess stood, only to have no idea whether to go to him or stay where she was. "Oh, Eli…I'm so sorry. You must've felt like your heart had been ripped out."

"Yeah, that pretty much covers it." He gave her a contrite smile. "Karmic payback for dumping you, I suppose."

"Don't *even* go there," she said softly, taking a step closer. "Did you ever hear from them again?"

"No."

The light dawned. "Which is why you don't date women with children."

He closed the gap between them, slowly lifting his hands to carefully bracket her jaw. "*Didn't* date women with children."

Tess froze. Then backed up, away from his touch, even if not from his gaze. Which Eli held in his as he said, "A couple days ago I had this, this epiphany, I guess you'd call it, about me needing to regain control of my life. Only I totally had the wrong end of the stick about what that meant. Because it occurred to me what I've been listening to all this time was fear. Fear of somethin' bad happening if…if I let myself get too close to someone. Especially someone with children. Except then, tonight, while I was holding Julia? I thought, screw this." Tess felt the blood drain from her face as he approached her again. "I'm done with being scared, with letting the past sit on my shoulder, sayin', *What makes you think you can have that?* With running from the very thing I most want."

"Eli…don't…"

But he'd once more taken her face in his hands, and damn, there went her knees again. "You know as well as I do," he said softly, caressing her cheeks with his thumbs, "that there's kissing and then there's *kissing.* When touching somebody is only about sex, and when it's about something else. And yeah, I know all about how you don't want this—" again, he grazed her lips with his, whispering into her mouth as tears crowded the corners of her eyes "—that maybe you don't want *me*—" this time his lips lingered a little longer, a little more firmly "—but the way I see it, what have I got to lose by saying I'd like to see where this goes—?"

"Eli? Tess?" his father's voice boomed from the doorway. "You in here?"

Eli caught Tess's freaked expression a split second before she backed away, stumbling slightly on those dumb boots of hers.

"Y-yes," she said to his dad, marching out front. "Is everything okay?"

The older man chuckled. "Why are those always the first words out of a mama's mouth?" he asked, holding the door open for her. "Everything's fine, but your little one just woke up and asked for you. No need to hurry," he said as Tess scurried past him. He tossed a half-assed wave at Eli, then followed her. "Donna's feeding her, everything's under control…"

Eli released a half laugh at his father's word choice. Control? There was a laugh. Yeah, he'd made a decent stab at conquering the fear he'd let govern him these past several years, and that felt good. But scaring Tess off hadn't exactly been part of the game plan.

She and the kids were gone by the time he got back to the house. No surprise there. Nor was the questioning look his mother lobbed at him, followed by a casual "Everything okay?" first chance she got, when everybody had gone home and Eli was helping her stack the chairs and what-all back in the frigid garage.

"Sure. Why wouldn't it be?"

"You tell me."

"Everything's fine, Mom," he said, giving her a fast hug before grabbing his jacket and walking out the open garage door and back to his own house.

He barely got inside before his cell rang. He stared at the display for a couple more rings, steeling himself, before he answered.

"I take it the kids are asleep."

"Yeah," Tess said, then heaved something between a laugh and a sigh. "I have absolutely no idea why I'm calling."

Eli lowered himself onto the edge of his sofa. "You do know who you called, right?"

This time the laugh had a little more oomph to it, the slightly hysterical twinge notwithstanding. "You do know *you* threw me a curveball tonight, right?"

"Yeah, sorry about that. But I had to, before I thought of all the reasons why I shouldn't. Except you know…I'm thinking this was more about me finally breaking through something I should've dealt with a long time ago than it was about you. You and me. Whatever."

"Really?"

"Really."

"That's not just you covering your butt?"

Eli smiled. "There might be some of that going on, but mostly no. So whatever you say, I'm good."

A pause. "You sure?" she said, and Eli told himself it was nuts to feel disappointed.

"I'm sure." When she hesitated again, though, his patience

kinda gave out on him. "Tess, for cryin' out loud—how long does it take to say 'No damn way—'?"

"That's not what I was going to say," she said softly.

"What?"

"Oh, Eli," she said on another sigh, and he could just see the what-am-I-about-to-get-myself-into? expression on her face. "Right now, right this moment, everything I said to you in the restaurant that day, about needing my autonomy—I still feel the same way. So by rights I *should* be telling you no damn way. But…I can't."

"And the problem with this is…?"

"The problem is, I don't know how much I've got left to give. If it would be enough for you." She hesitated again. "I care about you, I really do. What you told me tonight broke my heart. And made me see red, that somebody would lie to you like that. And…and when we're together, you make me feel…good. Almost hopeful. But…" She sighed. "I can't seem to think in terms of forever anymore. Not about you, I mean, I really can't fathom it. As if the concept itself doesn't compute."

"Then…" Eli took several deep breaths to calm his stampeding heart. "Then how about we just take it day by day?"

"But you've already been hurt once—"

"And I survived. Didn't think I would at the time, but I did." He leaned his head back on his sofa, his eyes shut. "And so did you."

The silence was almost deafening, so much so Eli was sure she was gonna say forget it, she'd changed her mind. Instead she whispered, after what seemed like an hour, "Day by day?"

"Day by day, honey," he said, adding, for good measure, "You call the shots."

"What about the kids?"

"Same goes. I can be as much or as little a part of their lives as you want." At her silence, he added, "But I won't let them get attached and then leave 'em high and dry."

"That's a pretty big promise."

"I know."

"And what do you get out of this?"

"You have to ask?"

She laughed softly. "Honestly, you sound like me trying to close a deal on a house."

"How'm I doing?"

Another lengthy pause preceded, "I'll leave the front porch light on."

Her hand shaking, Tess set her cell phone on the counter and crossed her arms over her equally quivering stomach, thinking, *You've gone and done it now, sister.*

Had she really just given the green light to a real, honest-to-God affair? The one-night boinkfest had been bad enough, a smirch on her otherwise-sainted life—she thought with a tight smile—she'd never live down, even if only in her own head.

But she was tired. Tired of always making the *right* choice, doing the *right* thing, always sacrificing her own needs for her children's.

And at least she'd been truthful with Eli. She wasn't sure she believed in forever anymore, except when it came to her babies—

Her phone rang. She picked it up, her heart thundering, half hoping he'd changed his mind, half apprehensive that he had.

"Got as far as Ortega's and realized I don't actually know where you live."

"Oh. Right. East on Main to Jefferson, then three blocks north. Car's in the driveway."

"Got it."

A couple of minutes was all she had to…do what? Call him back, say she'd had second thoughts? Slip into something less…motherly? She glanced down at her turtleneck and jeans, tried to remember what she was wearing underneath. Cotton cami and briefs. Pink. Boring—

She heard Eli's truck pull up behind her SUV, hurried to open the front door before he rang the bell. The cold air rushed in, balm to her heated face as she watched first one long leg then the other emerge from the cab. Once out, he slammed shut his door, setting the neighbor's dog to barking. A black Lab/rottie mix, as sweet as he was dumb. And loud.

"Sorry!" Eli whispered, cringing slightly as he tiptoed up the walk.

"It's okay," she said, eyes on his as he approached. "The kids sleep through anything."

"Glad to hear it," he murmured, taking her in his arms and kissing the very bejeezus out of her. For a moment, the fear blossomed, hot and red and fierce…only then Eli backed up, his hands on her shoulders, and smiled—not a full-out grin, just this tiny little how-ya-doing? tilt to his lips that made her laugh. She lifted her hands to his face, hard and scratchy and male, his soft curls tickling her knuckles, wanting him—wanting *forever*— so badly she thought she'd expire right then and there.

"You're cold," she whispered.

"Long as you plan on letting me in the house, shouldn't be a problem."

"I can do that," she said, taking him by the hand and leading him inside. A young fire popped and snapped in the kiva fireplace in the corner, bathing everything in rippling gold.

"This is nice," Eli said, quietly shutting the front door behind him and removing his cowboy hat, dropping it on the table beside him. "Sure different from my place."

"Yeah, but at least your place is real," tumbled out of her

mouth before she had a chance to catch it. Eli gave her a hard look. "What you see is from my what-can-I-do-to-save-my-marriage? phase. Because it felt, I don't know. Masculine. It's not really me, though."

"And what is you?"

"Honestly? I haven't had five minutes to figure it out."

"So maybe you should ditch everything you don't like until you do."

She laughed. "Just like that?"

"Why not? Why live with stuff that makes you feel like you're in somebody else's house? And that sectional would look real good in the Coyote house, don't you think?"

Tess turned, visualizing the pale leather against the brown sugar walls, and smiled. "Sold," she said, and Eli chuckled, saying he'd swing back by to pick it up after he delivered the bed and table the following day. Then he noticed the Christmas tree box leaning against the wall, surrounded by boxes of lights and ornaments she'd dragged in from the garage.

"You fixing to put up your tree?"

"Tomorrow. Give the kids something to do."

"Now's as good a time as any," he said, slipping off his jacket and tossing it over the sofa arm. "That way you and the kids can get to decorating it right away. Where you planning on putting it? Over against that wall? Or in front of the window? 'Course, if you do ditch the sofa I suppose you can put it pretty much anywhere you like—"

"For goodness sake, Eli—I didn't invite you over to put up my Christmas tree! I thought—" She stopped, blushing.

The tree freed from its coffin, Eli looked over at her. "I didn't come over to sleep with you," he said quietly.

"You…didn't."

"No, ma'am. Not tonight, anyway."

"Okay…did I miss something?"

"Tess…" He glanced down, a muscle working in his cheek, before looking at her again. "If I only wanted…that, I'd have no trouble finding a willing partner." When she choked back a laugh, he shrugged. "Just bein' honest. But that's not what I want from you. Let me rephrase that," he said, chuckling. "It's not *all* I want from you."

He stood and walked over to her, cupping her shoulders, and she shivered, and he smiled. A sweet, calm smile that tore her into itty-bitty pieces inside. "What I want," he said softly, "is a *relationship* with you. A real one. Somebody I can talk to, can talk *with*. Somebody who's cool with some-times just hanging out and puttin' up the Christmas tree. Sex…that's just the icing on the cake. Make no mistake—I love icing," he said, the grin widening. "The richer and sweeter, the better. But I got over eating it straight from the bowl a long time ago."

With that, he dropped a kiss on her forehead and went back to crouch in front of the dismembered tree. "So. You know where you want this?"

So not how she'd envisioned the evening. Nor did she expect to find herself more relieved than disappointed. "Um…over in that corner, I guess."

Ten minutes later, curled up on the sofa she now couldn't wait to see leave, watching the Big, Strong, Handsome Dude wrestle fake conifer branches into submission, she had to admit…it was nice, just talking, and sitting and marveling at this person in her living room, doing something for her *she wouldn't have to do.* Sure, her antennae tingled—along with other things—as she acknowledged the scenario's pitfalls, i.e. the voice murmuring, *Don't get used to this, honey.* But as the minutes ticked by, she could feel months of stress begin to seep from her body, even as her eyes grew heavier and her words slurred.

Eli glanced over, another smile toying with his mouth. "Sleepy?"

She yawned into the back of her hand. "Too much turkey. And stuffing and pecan pie and—" Another yawn. "Everything."

"So why don't you snooze for a few minutes while I finish this up?"

Even as she squished the throw pillow underneath her head, she mumbled, "What is it about you that always makes me pass out?"

Eli chuckled. And oh, my, was she growing fond of that chuckle...

The voices jolted her awake some time later. Eli's and Micky's. As she struggled out of sleep—and the throw Eli had apparently draped over her—she noticed the tree was not only up, but the red and gold garlands were strung. Eli and her son were both sitting on the floor in front of the fire, their backs to her, eating pie—Donna had insisted on sending home leftovers—and engaged in earnest conversation.

"And what are you doing out of bed, young man?" she said, sitting up.

Both heads turned to her. "I hadta pee," Micky said with a shrug, then grinned, cherry filling all over his face. "Look, Mama—Eli put the tree up!"

"I can see that."

Looking back at the lit tree, the boy sighed. "This has been the *best* day of my life. Can we start puttin' stuff on it now?"

"No," Tess said. "Tomorrow. Now you need to rebrush your teeth—and don't 'awww' me, you know you have to— and get back in bed."

"Go on, squirt," Eli said gently, cupping the back of Micky's head. "Do what your mama says."

Grumbling, Micky got to his feet and started toward the hall, then turned. "Can you come help us decorate the tree tomorrow?"

"I'd love to, big guy...but I got work to do getting the house ready for your mom, so she can show it to people on Saturday."

"It's okay, I understand," Micky said, wearing the same resigned expression he trotted out whenever his father pulled one of his "Gee, I'm so sorry, but I can't" tricks.

"Hey," Eli said, now on his feet, as well. "C'mere."

When Micky returned, Eli leaned over, a hand on the boy's shoulder. "I'm not blowing you off," he said gently, looking directly into her son's eyes. "I swear. I really am busy. But..." Eli looked at Tess. "If you need help putting up outside decorations, I could maybe swing by on Sunday?"

"Yes," Micky said with a fist bump, even as Tess sucked in a breath.

"There's no rush," she said, eye to eye, as deliberately as she could. "We have plenty of time. It's...another whole week until December."

One side of Eli's mouth kicked up. "You don't want to wait until it's too cold, though."

She paused. "I won't. I promise."

"What *are* you two talking about?" Micky said, his hands on his hips, and both of them burst out laughing.

"You, back to bed," Tess said, lightly swatting him on the rump. "And you," she said to Eli, "need to go home."

"Yes, ma'am," he said, ambling to the door as she kept an eye out to make sure her child actually made it all the way back to his bedroom. Eli didn't open the door, though, until she joined him there, when he leaned over and dropped a soft, slow kiss on her mouth, the kind of kiss that left her still slightly puckered when it was done, wanting more. "This has been one of the nicer days of my life, too," he murmured. "At least, by the end," he said with a grin and a wink, plunking his hat on his head. "'Night."

"'Night."

Tess stood at the door, watching him make his loose-limbed way down the porch steps, thinking, *It's okay, I can handle this,* immediately followed by, *Yeah, right.* Because for one thing she had no earthly clue what *this* even was. Or could be. Or, more important, what she wanted it to be. All she knew was, once he was gone, she missed him.

And that, boys and girls, was not a good sign.

*But no sense worrying about that today, Scarlett,* she thought on a sigh as she went back inside and shut the door. Right now she needed to concentrate on getting that house sold, not on grinning, good-looking ex-boyfriends determined to worm their way back into her life.

Her heart.

Just as she was putting the smeared pie plates into the dishwasher, Enrique called. "Hey," he said. "How's it going?"

Tess frowned. "It's…going fine."

"You and the kids have a good day?"

"Uh, yeah, I guess….Ricky, why are you calling?"

"Look, I know this is kinda last minute, and I know I missed Thanksgiving, but if you want I could still take the kids Saturday and Sunday."

"Well, actually…" *It's not about you, cookie, it's about them.* "Yeah, sure, that would be good, since I've got an open house on Saturday. But why'd you change your mind?"

A very long silence preceded, "Because there's somebody I'd like them to meet."

Eli had just settled in front of the TV with a DVD in the player and the cat on his lap when his cell rang. Seeing Tess's number, he nearly jumped out of his skin.

"Hey, there." *Breathe, breathe…* "What's up?"

"Um…never mind, this is dumb, pretend I never called. I mean, you're probably busy—"

"That's why some bright dude invented the pause button. Tess? Talk to me."

By this point his heart was going *whumpawhumpawhumpa* and his brain had taken off for parts unknown. For Tess to call him about anything…this was huge. Beyond huge. And, truth be told, more than a little scary.

"I just…I need somebody to vent to for a minute," she said. "Not dump on," she quickly added. "There's a difference."

"Goes without saying," Eli said, even though he was thinking, *There is?*

"It's just….Ricky just called. He wants to take the kids after all, on Saturday and Sunday. Because…" She cleared her throat. "Because he wants them to get to know his new girlfriend."

"Ouch."

"Yeah."

Stalling—because what the hell did he know?—Eli reached for the Coke sitting on his coffee table, uprooting the cat, who gave him the *You will so die* look and stalked to the other side of the couch. "You okay with that? The kids being with somebody you don't know, I mean?"

"Actually, I do know her. Sorta. A gal in the office where he works. I've talked to her a couple times. She seems…nice. Sweet. Ricky says she's got a little girl of her own."

"And you want to punch something, right?"

She let out a sharp, not-funny laugh. "This is stupid. I should be taking this a lot better than I apparently am."

Not what a guy falling hard for a woman wants to hear. Still, she'd called him, right? "Want me to come over?" he quietly asked.

"No," she said, sighing. "It's not that bad. *I'm* not that bad. It's just…it's history, you know? Why should I even care? And it's not as if I didn't expect this someday. But as soon as the words were out of his mouth…it was like all those feelings came rushing back."

"What feelings?"

Long pause. "That I failed. That I wasn't good enough."

"You do know that's a crock?"

"I didn't say it was logical. But thanks for the bitch slap. I needed that. Listen, I should let you get back to your movie—"

"It can wait, Tess—"

"No, really, I'm fine. I actually feel much better, I swear. So…thanks."

"But I didn't do anything."

She hesitated, then said, "You were *there,* Eli. That's…a lot. Well. Bye—"

"No, wait—how about I pick you up after the open house? We can go someplace for dinner. Maybe up to Santa Fe."

This pause was at least three times longer than the others. "You mean, like a date?"

"*Like,* nothing. I'm asking you out."

He heard her sharp intake of breath; Eli held his. "Okay, you're on. As long as you take me someplace where the meat isn't smothered by a half-inch of breading. And the dessert is guaranteed to instantly add five inches to my butt."

He chuckled. "I think that can be arranged. You want me to pick you up at the Coyote house?"

"No, I'll have to go back to the office afterward anyway, so why don't you just pick me up at home? Around six?"

"Six it is," he said, hanging up. Feeling smug.

Belly got up in his face again, glaring. *If it's not toooo much trouble, can we get back to what we were doing before we were so rudely interrupted?*

"You don't understand, cat," Eli said as she settled herself in his lap, giving him the goony face as she started kneading his thigh. "I just scored a Saturday night date with Tess Montoya."

Belly gave him a *Big whoop for you* look and resumed her kneading.

## Chapter Eleven

Maybe the cat wasn't so far off, after all, Eli mused irritably, sipping his after-dinner coffee across from Tess in the upscale Santa Fe restaurant and listening to her joke with the young server as the dude removed her practically licked-clean dessert plate. Because whatever gains he'd thought they'd made in regards to her being open with him seemed to have disappeared faster than her piece of Mississippi mud pie.

Not that he didn't understand how her experiences had bred a need to stay positive no matter what—especially for her kids' sakes. And he was reasonably sure she'd genuinely enjoyed herself this evening, if her reaction to the meal had been any indication. Man, the way she closed her eyes when she put that first bite of steak in her mouth? He half thought she was gonna lose it right there. Or he was, a memory that made him grin, despite his frustration. But—

"What?" Tess said, setting her coffee cup back in the

saucer, and Eli caught that damn sense of failure lurking behind her own smile, the one he'd finally begun to realize was always there to some degree, even when there was no cause. The one that put paid to this, this *act* that everything was fine when he knew damn good and well it wasn't.

*And nobody said this was gonna be easy, brainiac.*

"Just random thoughts passing through," he said, reminding himself he'd known going in what he was up against. Still, sheer orneriness made him ask, "You feeling better?"

Pressing her napkin to one corner of her mouth, Tess looked at him, years of self-preservation clouding the truth in her eyes. "About?"

"Take your pick. Enrique showing up with whatshername to pick up the kids, the open house being a bust."

Her mouth twisted. "I thought the whole purpose of this dinner was to make me forget all that."

"Big difference between easing the pain and pretending it's not there. Took me years to figure that out. Maybe because I wasted so much time fooling myself about who I was, what I wanted…" Eli lowered his eyes to his cup, then lifted them again. "I have a real low tolerance for fakes."

Not surprisingly, she bristled. "You think I'm a fake?"

"Obviously not or we wouldn't be here. And nobody understands better'n me why there's stuff that might be difficult for you to talk about. Why you feel you gotta put on the happy face for most people. But I'm not most people. I hope anyway. Tess…" He reached across the table to take her hand. "The only thing I want from you is honesty," he said, adding, after a short pause, "However that plays out."

Tess looked at him for another long moment, then smiled. "Okay, fine. I'm really, really bummed that not a single soul showed up for the open house."

"That's better," Eli said, leaning back. "And?"

"And I wanted to rip out whatshername's hair."

Eli picked up the salt shaker, tapping the bottom against the tablecloth. Maybe that was more information than he needed. "You're really that jealous?"

"Jealous? No! Just…pissed. That Enrique…" She blew out a breath. "That he can break all the rules, walk away and start all over again." Her mouth flattened, barely holding in the "Sorry" Eli knew was just behind her half-eaten-off lipstick.

"Tess." She lifted her eyes. "It's okay to be mad. About that, about the house, all of it. Being justifiably upset when things go wrong isn't the same thing as being negative on general principles. You don't have to pretend you're happy to keep your friends, okay?"

After a long moment, she nodded. "Okay."

"Although nobody can say the house wasn't a knockout," Eli said, steering the conversation into safer waters. "You never did tell me how you wrangled Aidan into lettin' you borrow some of his paintings. And the rugs."

"Oh," she said, relaxing some, "he'd thought the gallery in New York wanted twenty, but turns out—because some of them are so big—they only had room for sixteen. So he asked if I'd like to borrow the extras. Same with the rugs. He and June used to collect them, so he had way more than he and Winnie can actually use. I told Aidan if the place sells—"

"*When* it sells."

She rolled her eyes. "—I'll have to split the commission with him. It really did suck today," she added, sighing. "I didn't necessarily expect an offer right away, but not even the local lookie-loos came by. What's up with that?"

"You said yourself the Saturday after Thanksgiving wasn't a good time. So you try again."

"Oh, like people are going to be less occupied the closer

it gets to Christmas? As Suze so gleefully pointed out." Then she smiled. "You're right, this does feel good. Just stop me if I get too obnoxious, 'kay?"

"Deal," Eli said, lifting his cup in salute. "What is Suze's problem anyway? Doesn't she get a split of the commission from your sales?"

"The office does, not her. I work with her, not for her. She's just…" She sighed. "Strange."

Eli chuckled. "Tell me about it."

"She, um, tells me you two went out?"

Took a supreme effort not to let a smile slip at Tess's obvious discomfort with that idea, but Eli managed. "One date," he said, shrugging. "Ages ago. Although…" He smiled again, remembering. And, okay, deliberately provoking. "She hit on me up at the Lone Star a few weeks ago."

Tess's eyes darted to his. "And…?"

"And nothing. I don't find desperation attractive."

The instant the words left his mouth he realized his mistake, but not fast enough to head off Tess's "Oh, God—I must've *really* repulsed you that night."

"That was different."

"How?"

"Because it was you."

He saw her breath catch, felt her gaze melt into his as, in true chick-flick fashion, everything and everybody else seemed to melt around them—

"Can I get you folks some more coffee?"

"No, I think we're good," Eli said with a too-bright smile for the server as he reached for his wallet and Tess once again said how wonderful the meal had been. Eli noticed the young man's blush and almost laughed.

"We can split that, you know," she said after he disappeared, grabbing her purse.

"Over my dead body. I'm not a complete throwback. I do know how to take a gal on a date."

"Let me get the tip, at least—"

"Tess, honey…" Half smiling, he placed his credit card atop the bill. The waiter almost instantly whisked it away. "Would you please let somebody else take care of you for once?"

He saw her tear up. "I'm not sure I know how to do that."

"That's what I'm here for," he said, waggling his brows.

To his immense relief, she laughed.

A tiny thrill shot through Tess when Eli closed his strong, warm hand around hers, leading her across the restaurant's parking lot in the stunningly cold Santa Fe night. For a moment she warped back to a time when life was still fresh enough to slough off reality, to still believe in things like trust and safety and peace and hope. To believe in possibilities.

Eli plugged a CD into the truck's sound system, something mellow and jazzy.

"This okay?"

"Yeah, it's nice," she said, relaxing into her seat. Pretending to, at least. It occurred to her she had no idea what his musical taste was anymore, assuming—please God—he'd outgrown his grunge rock phase. The tempo picked up, Eli scatting softly along with it. She'd forgotten what a good voice he had—

"Did you know June?"

"Um, a little," Tess said, sitting up straighter, wondering why on earth he'd brought up Aidan Black's first wife. "Where'd that come from?"

"Just thinking about how gutsy she was." She could barely see his slight smile when he glanced over. "Wasn't hard to see why Aidan was so crazy about her. Or why her death hit him so hard. I'm sure he never in a million years thought he'd get a second chance like he did. With Winnie, I mean."

Thinking, *Oh, boy,* Tess said, "Is that what you want, Eli? A second chance with me?"

"Actually, no. Well, yeah, obviously I would, but…I wasn't talking about myself. It's you who deserves another shot, at love, at happiness, at whatever life's gypped you out of." Her own mind was whirling so much she didn't at first realize he'd paused. Until he said, "Whoever that's with isn't the issue."

Her heart pounding, she looked at Eli's profile, barely visible in the dark. "You honest to God mean that?"

"I honest to God do."

Approaching Tierra Rosa's outskirts—such as they were— they passed Garcia's market, the security lights in the parking light slashing across Eli's face, and for the first time Tess saw—*really* saw—the man he'd become.

The man she was falling in love with, God help her.

Her neighbor's doofus dog *bar-owfed* at them when the truck pulled into her drive. Shaking, one hand on the door latch, she considered her options. Considered, again, what she wanted versus what she *should* do. Oddly, the choices weren't nearly as cut-and-dried as she might have expected. Hoped they'd be. Finally, she swung her gaze to Eli, saw a tenderness in his expression that brought a lump to her throat. "Would you…like to come in?"

His lips tilted. "For coffee?"

"No."

He blew out a half laugh, half sigh. "I don't expect—"

"I know. And I wouldn't be making the offer if I thought you did."

The man just kept looking at her, like he was trying to see straight through her. Cowering under his scrutiny, she faced front again. "I'm trying, Eli. But I'm scared."

His seat creaked when he leaned across to gently touch her jaw, bringing her eyes back to his. "Of what?"

"You get one guess."

Releasing a breath, Eli sagged back in his seat, one hand on the steering wheel. "For however long you want me in your life," he said, turning to her again, "I'm here."

Her vision blurred. "Unfortunately, you're not the first person to say that to me."

"Yeah, but I mean it."

And oh, my, how she wanted those words to trample the fear welling up higher and higher inside her.

"Tess?" She looked over. "Whatever you want to do, I'm fine with it. Your call."

"I want you to come inside," she said.

After another long gaze, Eli got out and went around to her side to open her door, help her down from the truck. The door shut, he slipped one arm around her waist, sending another thrill through her, this time of eager, if bittersweet, anticipation. Behind a chain-link gate on her neighbor's side yard, the dog started whuffling and whining.

"What's his name?"

"Butch. He's a complete wuss."

"Be right back," Eli said, releasing her to go see the dog, who became unhinged with joy. Crouching, he shot the breeze with the beast for a minute while Tess unlocked the front door, joining her by the time she'd dumped her purse and keys on the entry table, then turned on the lamp by the chintz floral sofa sitting where the sectional had been.

"Nice chat?"

Eli shut the door behind him. "Butch wasn't real keen on money markets these days, said my safest bet would be in Treasury bonds."

Laughing over her knotted stomach, Tess plopped onto the pink monstrosity, nearly turning herself inside out to get her boot off.

"Um, wow," Eli said, frowning at the sofa. "Flowers. And…ruffles."

She twisted in another direction, but the boot wouldn't budge. "Thea and Jonny brought it over yesterday so there'd be someplace to sit—it came with the ranch when he inherited it—but it's like having Miss Piggy in my living room. She won't be staying."

"I feel much better now," Eli said, undoing his bolo tie as he approached. "Need help?"

"No, no…I've got it…whoa!"

Her butt slid forward when Eli grabbed her foot, yanking off the boot in one swift move, then motioned for the other. When she frowned, one side of his mouth slid up and her mind shorted out for a sec. "Think of it as foreplay."

"In that case—" up went the other tootsies "—have at it…oops!"

Her hand flailed out, knocking the remote off the end table. Eli got to it before she did, then dropped onto the sofa beside her. Really close. Omigod-I-want-to-eat-you-up-you-smell-so-good close. "So," he said, wiggling the remote. "Still don't know how to use this?"

"Sure I do. I just keep poking at things until something happens."

"Sounds a lot like my first sexual experience."

"Yeah, I do seem to remember a lot of trial and error going on there."

The remote clutched in his hand, Eli looked at her, their mouths *really* close. "Was it that awful?"

"If you're asking me if rockets went off…no." Tess hesitated, then let her hand stray to his shirt buttons. Sober—she hadn't even had wine with dinner—she was strangely shy. "But it wasn't awful."

"I know what buttons to push now," he said. "Which you may have noticed."

"You're killing me here."

"That was the idea," he said, leaning closer. If that was possible. "Okay, to just turn on the TV…you hit this…then this…"

The TV blooped to life. Tess reared back to gawk at Eli. "You're giving me a remote tutorial *now?*"

"Yep."

"Why?"

"Because you need to know how this thing works. So." He smacked the remote into her hand, then hauled her foot into his lap and started massaging her instep. Oh, *mama*. "You do it."

"While you're doing…that?"

"Just gettin' you nice and warmed up—"

"You're not just teasing me?"

His eyes bore into hers. Dead serious eyes. Dead serious, sexy-as-hell eyes. "I don't tease, honey. Now go on," he said, nodding at the TV. "Show it who's in charge."

Suddenly realizing she might well come out of the evening with both a teeth-rattling orgasm *and* the ability to program her DVR, Tess did indeed play along, until Eli at long last—meaning, maybe five minutes later—pronounced her Queen of the Comcast remote, and as a reward, she supposed, moved in for a kiss that could've supplied power for the entire town, it was that slow and delicious and thorough. But when she reached for the hem of her sweater, he shook his head.

"Nope, not yet."

"Because…?"

"Because what's the rush?" He kissed her again, easing her back onto the sofa.

"You just wanna make out and stuff?"

"For now," he said, smiling. Stroking her temple with his

thumb. His lips touched hers, just enough to stir things deep inside her, not enough to make them boil over. Yet. "We had sex. Now I want to make love to you. For as long as it takes. And in my book, making love means lots of kissing…long, slow, wet kissing…"

Not a tease. Right.

"Um," she said as his mouth lowered to her neck, "any reason we can't do this…um…n-naked?"

"You know," he murmured between kisses along her jaw, "you really need to learn how to relax and enjoy the moment."

"I'm thinking I'd enjoy it a lot more naked. On six-hundred count cotton sheets."

Chuckling, Eli pushed himself to his feet, then pulled her up, as well. "Whatever you want, sweetheart," he said, tugging her into her bedroom and turning on the lamp beside the bed, the bedroom all in neutral colors because that's what Enrique liked, never mind that she'd always dreamed of cobalt-blue walls and crisp white linens—

*No, Teresa,* she heard her mother say, *you can't paint the walls blue. It's too hard to paint over them again if we sell the house…*

"Hey," Eli whispered, bracketing her face with his hands, concern vibrating in his eyes. "Where'd you go?"

"Sorry, I… It's nothing." She smiled, wondering why, *why,* she constantly sabotaged herself, why it *was* so damned hard to simply enjoy the moment?

*Because that's all it ever is. A moment.*

"Undress me," she whispered, and he did, pressing his mouth to her belly and collarbone and shoulders as each item of clothing bit the dust, then removing his own clothes as she lay on the bed, watching. Trembling. Finally naked, Eli slid beside her to pull her close, not hard, not frantically, but with a deliberateness that turned her bones to water, made her mold to all that solid warmth like Silly Putty. "Tonight," he said softly into her hair, making her sigh when he palmed her breast, "it's all about you. What you want. What*ever* you want."

Once again, tears crowded her eyes. But she blinked them away before smiling up at him. "You're sure brave," she said lightly, knowing instantly he wasn't buying her act for a single moment. And it rattled her all over again, how this man could see straight through to where she was most raw, most vulnerable, giving him more power over her than anyone else had ever had. Not Enrique, not her mother…no one.

But for all that, it was her night. *Her* moment, fleeting thought it might be…a night when she didn't have to meet anyone's expectations but her own. With that, she pulled out of his arms and turned off the light, leaving the room bathed in stark, silvery-blue moonlight.

Because she couldn't bear to see his face, see the one thing in his eyes she didn't dare trust…couldn't bear for *him* to see, when he filled her, how empty she still felt.

The heat kicking on startled Eli awake; took him a few seconds to fight off the slight disorientation, until his eyes adjusted to the cottony, predawn light and he realized the soft, fragrant weight against his chest was Tess. Except the crushing sensation inside his chest had nothing to do with her weight.

Careful not to disturb her, he lifted his watch from the nightstand, squinting at it. Six-thirty on a Sunday morning, the rest of the day entirely theirs, if they wanted it to be. If she wanted it to be. Except he'd known even before they'd walked into the house she'd been coiling more and more into herself, saying one thing and feeling something else entirely.

Not that there'd been anything even remotely forced about her trembling responses to his touch, her eagerness for him to explore and taste and love every inch of her body—as heartbreakingly tender as the encounter had been, she'd given, and taken, with an almost brutal honesty. But even Eli could sense the sadness beyond the gasps and murmurs of pleasure, the soft laughs and *pleases* and *yeses* and *like thats* that had driven him insane with wanting to please her, to possess her, to make her come like she never had before.

Since he hadn't exactly checked his Macho Club membership card at the door or anything.

Even after all that, though, he could see in the gradually lightening room the worry lines between her brows. The regret. And it killed him that he had no idea how to erase them. To make everything all right.

To make *her* all right, to undo years of broken promises and betrayals.

It also about killed him to ease himself out of the warm bed, but he couldn't think with her beside him like that, making him want her again. After taking care of morning business, he silently gathered his clothes and carried them out to the living room and got dressed, spying the boxes of outside decorations piled beside the haphazardly decorated Christmas tree. She'd let the kids do it, she'd said. He smiled at the chaotic jumble of ornaments, how she'd put aside her own borderline OCD issues for her kids.

By now, the sliver of sky peeking through the closed drapes was a thin, milky-gray—light enough for his purposes. Eli started a pot of coffee and slipped on his coat, then carted the boxes outside into the silent, frigid morning. The decorations seemed easy enough, he thought as he buttoned up his coat and pulled on his gloves—some icicle lights, three or four strands of big colored bulbs, all painstakingly wrapped around little plastic forms. The no-fuss, no-muss choices of a single parent with too many things to do and too little time to do them.

A half hour later, the front door swung open. Hair sticking up in a thousand directions, her arms folded over a fuzzy, light purple robe that made her look like a leftover Easter chick, Tess blinked up at him, shielding her eyes from the now-bright sun. "What on earth are you doing?"

"Freezing my butt off. Hope you appreciate it."

The worry lines softened some when she smiled. "Are you kidding? Done is beautiful. Thanks." She returned his kiss when he climbed down off the stepstool he'd found in her garage, her fingers loitering at the nape of his neck, her eyes not quite meeting his when he pulled back. "Wow," she said. "All this and coffee, too?"

"See how handy I am to have around?"

The smile faltered. "What would you like for breakfast? I picked up some bacon the other day, and I make a mean omelet. Three kinds of cheese, tomatoes, peppers, chile—whatever you like."

"All of the above?"

"You got it," she said, shuffling toward the kitchen.

Eli hauled the empty boxes back inside, letting them drop onto the floor before joining Tess in her immaculate kitchen, the regimented order even more pronounced in the sunlight streaming through the window over the sink.

"Need help?" he said to her back as she pulled eggs and cheese and bacon out of a sleek black fridge.

Still not looking at him, she shook her head. Eli let it go…until, after laying several strips of bacon in a cast-iron skillet, the egg she tried to crack into a glass bowl slipped out of her shaking hand, exploding on the tile floor.

"No, it's okay, I've got it," she said when he went for a paper towel.

"What you've got," he said, gently shoving her aside to clean up the slimy mess, "is a major case of B.S." Still squatting, he looked up at her, immediately saw the truth and chagrin in her eyes. "Didn't I tell you last night the one thing, the only thing, I want from you is honesty? So if you don't mind—" he got up to toss the soaked towel into her garbage, then rinsed off his hands "—I'd really appreciate you cutting the crap and telling me what's going on."

After a long pause, she said, very softly, "I don't want to ruin last night."

Eli turned, his heart splitting at her tormented expression. "Not possible."

The bacon began to hiss in the pan; she returned to the stove to turn down the heat, not even protesting when Eli took over egg-cracking duty.

"Okay," she said at last. "You want honesty? When I woke up and realized you weren't in bed, saw your clothes weren't there, I felt like somebody'd thrown me under a truck."

Squelching the spurt of irritation, Eli took a fork to the eggs to beat them into a froth. "So you still don't trust me."

Knuckling the space between her brows, Tess drifted over to the small kitchen table to sit in the chair facing the window, squinting into the sun. "This isn't about you."

"It was me in the bed with you last night, Tess. So how can it *not* be about me?"

Her eyes squeezing shut, she leaned forward, thrusting both hands through her messy hair for a second or two before tilting her eyes to his. "You remember telling me that you dumped me because you were scared of your feelings? That it was all too fast, too much, and you just couldn't deal?"

"I was seventeen, for God's sake."

Their gazes tangled for a second before she got up to turn the bacon. "Don't recall terror being age-specific."

"You're afraid of me?"

"You're not listening." Carefully setting down the fork, she turned. "I'm feeling things for you I haven't felt for anybody else in a long time," she said, her voice too soft, too controlled, "and I'm scared because…"

The corners of her mouth curved down. "Because except for my children, loving people has just never ended well for me, okay? My father left, my mother couldn't have cared less about me, my husband…" Tears bloomed in her eyes; he watched her blink them back. "I don't know…maybe there's only so many times a heart can get broken before it doesn't heal anymore—"

"Honey—"

"I was just beginning to feel safe, Eli, in this little world I've patched together from the scraps I've been left. You have no idea what a relief it is not having to worry about whether somebody loves me or not, or wonder why nothing I do seems to work. Don't you get it, Eli? I was finally *free*. And then you came along," she continued, close enough now to smack the heel of her hand on his shoulder, "with all these promises in your eyes, making me want to believe in something I'm absolutely petrified to believe in again—"

Tess twisted away, gripping the edge of the stove. "I think it's terrific that you were able to move past your heartbreak, but…" She shook her head. "I'm not there. And I don't know that I ever will be. I'm sorry, Eli," she whispered, hunched over. "But I don't know how to fix what's broken inside me. And I can't be who you or anybody else wants me to be. Not anymore."

Not quite sure how he was breathing, Eli reached around to move the popping bacon to the back burner, then wrapped an arm around her waist and pulled her back against his chest. "Then *you* don't get it," he said softly. "Because you already are who I want. You don't have to do a blessed thing except just be yourself. Now," he said, setting her aside and returning the pan to the still-hot burner, "you like your bacon crisp or chewy?"

Tess stumbled slightly, then frowned at him. "What?"

"Crisp or chewy?"

"No, I mean…" She wrenched a paper napkin out of a plastic holder by the stove and blew her nose. Sniffed again. "Why aren't you already out the door?"

Deciding the bacon was as done as it was gonna get, Eli lifted out each slice and set it on a wad of paper towels to drain. "Because I haven't had my breakfast yet," he said, setting the plate of bacon in the center of the table, "So you want to make these omelets or should I just scramble up a mess of eggs in this grease and call it good?"

Instead of answering, Tess slowly moved in to thread her arms around his ribs and lay her head on his chest, where she stayed so long the bacon got cold. But it wasn't an *It's okay* hug. Not by a long shot.

What it was, was the kind of hug you give somebody when you're saying goodbye.

## Chapter Twelve

"Honestly, you boys will drive me to an early grave yet," Eli's mother said on a what-did-I-do-to-deserve-this? sigh as she plunked a huge slice of warm, fragrant apple pie in front of him. "How *do* you get yourselves into these messes?"

What Eli couldn't figure out was how he'd gone to the house to pick up something for his father and ended up spilling his guts about Tess to his mother. Most of it anyway. The parts a guy can share with the woman who birthed him. Who, Eli had no doubt, was perfectly capable of filling in the missing pieces on her own.

Ironically, if it hadn't've been for the whole Tess fiasco, the past couple of weeks would have been okay. Business was picking up again, from both repeat customers and a few folks who'd seen his stuff when Tess or other agents had shown the Coyote Trail house. And it'd felt good, getting back to doing what he felt born to do. But the chasm growing between him and Tess—they'd barely even seen each other since the "sleep-over"—was killing him, plain and simple.

He forked in a bite of pie, mumbling, "At least I finally got the message that my 'being there' for Tess was having the exact opposite effect I'd intended. Instead of reassuring her, it's just making her feel crowded. So I'm backing off."

Sighing, his mother sat in the chair opposite his, concern brimming in her dark eyes. She'd been baking all day, evident by her messy face and hair. "Has she *said* she loves you?"

"No." Eli's mouth thinned. "But when she looks at me…" Blowing out a breath, he stuffed another chunk of pie in his mouth before rattling the fork onto the plate. "Dammit, Mom—I feel like the densest person on the planet. What am I missing?"

His mother tapped her fingers on the table for a couple of seconds, then said, "Honey, there's two kinds of people—the ones who never give up hope, no matter how many times they get screwed over, and the ones whose hurt goes so deep they can't trust a good thing even when it's right in front of their noses. From what you've told me, I'm guessing Tess is a card-carrying member of the second group."

"But she wasn't always like that! When we were in school, she was the funniest, most outgoing gal you'd ever want to meet."

"And did it ever occur to you all that was a mask for how she was really feeling?" his mother said gently. She sank her chin in her hand, pressing stray crumbs off the vinyl tablecloth with the pad of her thumb and releasing them onto Eli's plate. "I remember, when you'd bring her over here all those years ago, how she'd watch us like we were some kind of crazy reality show. Half of her was appalled, but the other half…oh, my, those big, brown eyes were filled with *such* longing. I was so mad at you for pulling that fast one on her, knowing how tender her heart was. Not that I didn't understand things from your point of view," she said at Eli's jerk. "But that didn't stop me from aching for her anyway."

Eli leaned back, his arms crossed over his chest. "Did you know her mother?"

"Not really, no. Marie was one of those women not inclined to put herself out there. Still. If I'd had any idea…" Another sigh. "My take on it is that Tess might be *coping* fine, just as she has all along. That gal has a spine of steel. But now you're asking her to trust something that's always let her down before. To take a huge leap of faith. If she's not ready to do that, there's nothing you or anybody else can do or say to convince her otherwise. Just like…"

"What?"

"Look how long it took you to get over that gal in Taos, to even think about dating a woman with children. So you know yourself that you can't rush these things. If she needs time, all you can do is give it to her."

"Says the woman who tried to fix up her own son with Sally Perkins."

"And when it didn't take, I let go. I do know how to bow out gracefully."

Eli chuckled, then released a breath. "And if Tess doesn't come around?"

His mother curled her fingers around his hand. "All you can do is let her know she's in your thoughts, that you care. Anything more gets into stalking territory," she said with a slight smile. "But you know, if it's meant to be, nothing can stop it. And if not…" Shrugging, she got up to cover the pie. "Then the dear Lord must have something even better for you." She turned. "And trust she's hearing the same voice you are. Prayer's not about asking, Elijah," Mom said before he could open his mouth. "It's about *listening*."

Definitely not what Eli wanted to hear, even if his mother's words nagged at him all the rest of the day and on into the evening. Especially the part about how long it'd taken him to move past *his* fears, which sure as heck had seemed valid enough to him. And not all that long ago, either. So who was he to judge whether or not Tess's were justified? Especially considering what he'd gone through didn't even compare with her experience.

He was still pondering all this when he swung by the Lone Star after making a delivery before heading home. The place was all gussied up for Christmas in colored lights and tacky tinsel garlands inside and out; the original Bobby Helms "Jingle Bell Rock" blared from the jukebox, adding to the holiday cheer. And good Lord, Ramon was wearing a Santa hat. Eli chuckled in spite of himself.

"Real fetching."

"Wife made me do it. Said it'd bring in business." He shrugged, a man who'd learned, after thirty years of marriage, to just go with the flow. "Tap okay?"

"Sure—"

"Well, look who the wind blew in," Eli heard beside him, and he thought, *Why me?* Wearing something revealing and sparkly, Suze stretched for the bowl of peanuts. "Oh, don't get that look on your face. I'm waiting for somebody, if you must know."

"Glad to hear it." In more ways than one.

"So what's up with you and Tess?" When Eli flinched so hard he nearly spilled his beer, Suze barked out a laugh. "Hot damn, I was right! You two *are* an item."

Eli frowned. "She say something?"

"Tess?" Suze blew out a short laugh, then tossed back a couple of peanuts. "Honey," she said, making a funny face when a piece of peanut went down the wrong way, "that gal wouldn't talk about her private life if you lit a fire under her feet. I, however, have remarkable powers of observation. So. What's going on?"

"Nothing." Suze snorted. Eli knocked back a swallow of beer and shook his head. "What I mean is, it never got off the ground."

"Huh," she said, picking the last nut from her palm, then brushing her hands together. "Only reason I asked is because she's been real tetchy this past couple of weeks. Nothing seems to cheer her up. Even though—you probably don't know this—I landed a major listing for a bunch of condos up in Taos that need some serious remodeling—God save me from eighties mauve and blue—" she shuddered "—so I was able to find jobs for those two carpenters she nearly drove me nuts about."

He frowned. "Teo and Luis?"

"That's right. Something about how the younger one was thinking the military was looking better and better as his path to financial security, unless he could find more work. It's a big job, should keep 'em employed at least through the spring."

Smiling, Eli lifted his beer to her. "Thank you," he said, thinking, *Yeah, just what I need—a reason to fall more in love with the woman.*

Suze shrugged. "No skin off my nose. But Tess would *not* let up until she knew I'd put the contractor in touch with them. I think she was worried more about that than the house not selling."

"Still?"

"You kidding? This time of year? Honey, we'd be talking Christmas miracle for sure if it did. Oh, there's my date… Lord, look at me with peanut bits all over *my* bits," she said, laughing and swiping at herself as she slid off the stool and into the crowd.

"I know I said I was gonna spend the night in Santa Fe,"

said a vaguely familiar, deep male voice behind him. "Changed my mind. There's a little B and B not far from here. It'll do for now…"

God, why did he know that voice? Eli casually glanced over his shoulder to catch a glimpse, but the guy was facing away. Broad back. Dark blond, shaggy hair. White cowboy hat on the table.

"…and I told you, I'm sick of Nashville. It's not home. Never was…. Yeah, I thought so, too, when I was twenty. I was wrong." He laughed. "Y'know, Al, strange as it might seem, not everything's about you…. When have I ever said I was ungrateful for everything you've done for me? I just need to get back to my roots is all. To recharge. And anyway, it's all over the Internet, how you just signed that hottie from one of those reality shows, so why on earth would you still need an old warhorse like me?"

Sipping his beer, the man turned, although Eli'd long since figured out who he was. Hell, Eli had a whole stack of Cash Cochran's CDs, even his first album right after Cash'd burst onto the Nashville scene. He'd almost forgotten the singer'd been born and raised right here—

"…not anticipating a problem, it's a buyer's market up here, same as it is everywhere else. Just have to hook up with a Realtor and I'm good." The country star chuckled. "Now you know why I refused to let those finance geniuses talk me into investing in the stock market. At least I still got my money… No, sir, I am not promising anything to anybody. Did that for more than half my life. Now it's all about me, what *I* want for a change."

His foot jiggling on the barstool rung, Eli frowned at his glass, telling himself it was none of his business, the man could find a house on his own, there was no way he could approach him without looking like some stupid fan….

Cochran stood and tossed some bills on the table, then headed for the door. Eli sprang from the stool, catching up with the other man in the small parking lot outside, patches of leftover snow from the day before glowing red from the Christmas lights, like God had spilled His Slurpee.

"Excuse me?"

The singer turned, a mixture of curiosity and annoyance glittering in his famous silver eyes. Eli held up his hands. "Sorry, don't mean to butt in, but I couldn't help but over-hear… I take it you're lookin' for a house?"

The man relaxed. "Might be. Why? You lookin' to sell one?"

"Not me. A…friend of mine. It's no mansion, but it's got four bedrooms and really pretty views. Real private, too. Here…" He handed over Tess's card, an old one still showing her with long hair. "That's the Realtor. Ask her about the Coyote Trail place. Of course, she can show you other houses, too, if that one doesn't work for you."

The man angled the card to get a better look in the red glow. "Tess Montoya. Pretty gal. Thanks," he said, tucking the card in his jacket pocket. "And who shall I say recommended her?"

"Doesn't matter," Eli said, backing toward his own truck. "Doesn't matter at all."

Fortunately for Tess, everybody had been so crazy busy with kid stuff and work stuff and, Christmas stuff it was halfway into December before her girlfriends and aunt were able to get together to hear about Florita's and Winnie's Excellent Adventure. Not that it still hadn't taken a supreme effort for Tess to drag her butt—and the two little butts she'd spawned—to Winnie's and Aidan's glass-and-wood mountain hideaway, but begging off would have only brought on a barrage of questions. Especially from her aunt, who Tess had avoided since Flo's return like a bad eighties mixed tape.

Because those eyes, they *saw things*…things Tess did not want Flo, or the three irritatingly cheerful, happily married women currently oohing and ahhing over Winnie's and Flo's Big Apple haul, to see.

While the menfolk attached to the women watched over assorted little people downstairs, the estrogenized among them congregated in Winnie's huge, cathedral-ceilinged bedroom with its star-studded skylights, the cheerful fire snapping and hissing in the eight-foot-tall stone fireplace. Rachel, Thea's nineteen-year-old stepdaughter, sprawled on her stomach across Winnie's patchwork-quilt-covered, four-poster bed, while Thea sat cross-legged beside her, stuffing her face with various goodies brought back from the Land to the East. Beside *her* lay Annabelle, Winnie's Border collie, all *verklempt* that Thea was, just at the moment, too distracted by her new hot-pink leather Kate Spade handbag to rub the dog's fluffy white tummy.

"Oh my word, Winnie—I cannot believe you did this!" Laughing, Thea hugged the bag to her stomach. "But I'm sure glad you did!"

"And these earrings are incredible," Rachel said, flicking back a stripe of hair the same color as Thea's new bag to reveal the cascading, interlocking gold loops. "Thanks!"

Curled up in a velvet armchair in front of the fire, Tess couldn't stop stroking the soft-as-a-baby's-cheek pashmina stole she'd just unwrapped. "Nobody expected you to bring us presents, you know."

"Like I was gonna go to New York and not?" Winnie said with a laugh, still the same skinny, blue-jeaned country gal who'd blown into town from West Texas two years ago, despite her husband's becoming one of the art world's rock stars. "There's gifts for all the kids, too, but they can't open theirs until Christmas. And," she said, her straight, shoulder-length dark blond hair gleaming red-gold in the firelight, "that's not all."

Amid protests from the other women, Winnie pulled three little boxes from an aqua Tiffany's bag she'd been hiding in her closet. Holding the boxes to her chest, Winnie blushed and said, "I only hope these make as much sense to y'all as they did to me. But not ever really having girlfriends before I came here, I wanted some way to show how much our friendship means to me."

She handed out the boxes, waiting until everyone else opened theirs before tugging out her own tiny, perfect silver teardrop pendant from underneath her Henley sweater. "Before somebody asks me what on earth I was thinking, giving y'all teardrops…" She blew out a breath. "Friendship's all about sharing tears, of joy and laughter as well as heartbreak. And I'm more grateful than I can say to have found y'all to share those tears with."

"Omigod, Winnie," Thea said, grinning and holding up her hair while Rachel fastened the pendant, then twisting to the do the same for the younger woman. "They're *perfect*. I am never, ever taking this off—"

"So what do you think?" Flo said, popping out of Winnie's master bath in something short and tight and gold, her own teardrop softly glimmering against her breastbone. "Hot, right?"

As the women all laughed, giving Tess's aunt a thumbs-up, Tess fingered the smooth, cool teardrop, her eyes stinging as she realized how much this little group meant to her, too. How much she loved them all.

And she knew they loved her.

The first sob exploded out of nowhere, followed by another, and another and another. After a moment of shared shock, at least two sets of arms cradled her shoulders, the other two women at her knees, holding her hand or patting her legs, everybody talking at once.

"Omigod, honey…what is it?"

"Annabelle, no, she doesn't need your sympathy—"

"Dude, eww…you're all snotty…let me get you a tissue—"

"An' maybe we should all jus' shut up and let the woman talk, you know?" Flo said, crouching beside her. No small feat in that outfit. "What happened, *carina?*"

So out it all came, the whole miserable story, that here was this good, kind man offering her everything she'd ever wanted and she was petrified to take it and how messed up was that? When she was done—feeling a lot like the time when, as a kid, she'd eaten way too much junk at the State Fair and had barfed it all back up at two in the morning, her first and last experience with puking—she realized the room practically vibrated with the silence. Her mouth pulled tight, she blew her nose.

"Now I remember why I don't do this."

"Do what?" Winnie asked, frowning.

"Dump on my friends."

"Oh, geez," Thea said, rolling her eyes from the edge of the bed, where she'd returned to hear out the tirade. "Don't make me come over there and smack you—"

"If I don' get there first," Flo said, then turned to the others. "Anyone up for hearing some of the background about this, raise your hands."

"Flo, for God's sake," Tess said as three hands shot up. But she had about as much chance of stopping the woman as she would an earthquake. Flo turned back to Tess, shaking her head. "Even as a little girl you always had this big heart, you know? Always wanting to give, give, give. I sometimes think it was only because your heart was so big that you survived at all."

"Did I?"

"Ha!" Thea erupted as Flo said, "Oh, my, yes. And then some. But as you got older, I could see caution start to take root in your eyes, even if not at first in your heart. Even now, you're good at pretending everything's fine when underneath your heart is breaking."

"Ain't that the truth?" Thea said, and Tess glared at her.

"How come?" Winnie asked, even though understanding was already blossoming in her clear blue eyes.

"Because the alternative was going under," Tess said softly, explaining about her father's leaving, her mother's lack of involvement.

"Damn, honey," Thea said. "I had no idea things had been that bad." She looked up at Flo. "Couldn't you have taken her when she was a kid?"

"You have no idea how much I wanted to," Flo said, stunning Tess with the depth of pain in her eyes. "But your uncle…he said no. That it wasn't our problem. An' then we moved away, an'…" Tears bulged in her eyes. "I'm so sorry. I feel like I let you down—"

"Don't be ridiculous," Tess said, grabbing her aunt's hand. "If anything, you were a lifeline. Even if only over the phone. And in any case—"

"I wasn't your mama."

"No. You weren't."

"Wait a minute," Rachel, who'd been dead silent all this time, finally said. The teenager's confused, angry eyes darted between Tess and her aunt. "Are you saying your mother didn't *want* you?"

Thea swatted her. "Rach, honestly—"

"And your father walked out when you were a kid, right? Holy heck, that's like almost exactly what happened to my dad! And it seriously messed him up for a long time. You know, about love and stuff," she said, aiming a quick grin at her stepmother before returning her gaze to Tess's. "Man, Tess, Flo's right—you're freaking amazing."

"Yeah," Tess said bitterly, slumping back in the chair with Annabelle's head on her lap. Absently, she stroked the dog's silky head, her mouth pulled down at the corners. "So freaking amazing that I..."

"Believe you can't trust love?" Flo said, her arms crossed over all that gleaming goldness. "That Eli is too good to be true? That..." She gripped the arm of the chair to look into Tess's eyes. "That you don' feel worthy of being loved?"

"No!" Tess said, rearing back. Then her mouth twisted. "I don't think."

Flo sighed. "When you told me about Eli—way back when, I mean—I was angry for you, that your first love should end so badly—"

"Your *first* love?" Winnie said, frowning.

"I'll fill you in later," Thea whispered.

"—but what *Enrique* did to you..." Flo straightened, arms crossed, brows plunged nearly as much as her neckline. "Him, I was furious with. I know you saw him as your Prince Charming. To be honest, I saw it, too. I remember thinking, *finally,* somebody worthy of my precious girl."

"Yeah," Tess said. "Me, too." She shrugged, taking in her audience. "Made it kinda hard to admit my marriage was falling apart."

"Boy, can I relate to that," Thea muttered, sighing.

From where she sat on the rug in front of the footboard, Winnie sent Thea a sharp look, then faced Tess again, frowning. "But things were still okay when you had Julia, right? I mean, I was there. You were so worried about Enrique making it back okay."

"Yeah, well," Tess said, sighing. "You tell yourself what you want to believe. And I didn't know then he was cheating on me."

"Bastard is *so* dead," Thea said over the others' collective gasp. Annabelle jumped to her feet, ready to save the day, as Flo cupped Tess's face with hands reeking of fancy moisturizer.

"An' you thought the baby would save the relationship, didn't you?"

"Lord, this is serious déjà vu time," Thea said, as Tess said, "Guess I thought it was worth a shot—"

"You know," Winnie said, "all this is really interesting, but it seems to me y'all are missing the point." She looked directly at Tess. "There's only one question you need to be askin' yourself—do you love the man?"

"It's not that simple."

"Yeah, it is. Do you or don't you?"

"It's like…I want to, but I can't."

"Can't? Or won't let yourself because you're afraid?"

"Same thing."

"No, not the same thing at all." This from Thea. "Trust me, I've been there, too. Not to mention that sobbing thing we all just witnessed? Not the action of somebody who only *wants* to love somebody. Honey, you may as well admit it—it's too late. You're *gone.* So you gotta ask yourself…which would be worse? Taking another chance?" She shrugged. "Or not taking it?"

"Is that a trick question?"

"Can I say something?" Rachel said, lifting a black-finger-nailed hand. "For what it's worth, Tess—Jess thinks the world of his brother. When everybody else was having five fits when we got pregnant and we weren't married or anything? Eli was the one who talked the rest of his family down. He also was the one who talked *Jesse* down, making him see he couldn't run away from his responsibility just because he was scared."

She wriggled off the bed to squat in front of Tess again, all earnest eyes and newly pierced eyebrow. "Eli's one of the good ones, Tess. Really. And yeah, I've heard the stories, too, that maybe he hadn't always made the best decisions in the past...but people overcome their pasts every day. I mean, dude—look around you!" she said, her gaze taking in Winnie and Thea. "Everybody's got crap to overcome, you know? So what's stopping *you?*"

*Oh, you're so young,* Tess thought as her phone rang.

Frankly grateful for the reprieve, she excused herself to take the call. Hustling into Winnie's bathroom, she shut the heavy wood door, glancing at the number. No name, unfamiliar area code.

"Tess Montoya speaking—"

"Yes, Ms. Montoya. Name's Cash Cochran—"

Her heart stopped.

"—and I'm sorry to be calling so late, but I was told to ask you about the house up on Coyote Trail...?"

Between her group therapy session with her girlfriends and Cochran's call, Tess hadn't slept worth squat the night before. But now the glittery pinons, the snow-frosted house against the clear, deep blue sky—like something right off an old-fashioned Christmas card—settled her racing heart at least enough to function.

The unexpected call had so stunned her she'd been doing well to make the viewing appointment. Only after she hung up did she realize Cochran hadn't asked anything about the house, nor had she volunteered any information. When she'd apologized that afternoon after meeting him at the property, he'd only chuckled in that famous low voice of his and said it didn't matter, that words couldn't tell a person, anyway, if something was right or not. That he'd only ask questions if he had 'em, after he'd walked through the house on his own.

Now crisp, snow-scented air blasted through the room as

he reentered through the new French doors, his expression blank as he stomped snow off his boots onto the mat Tess had just put there. Acknowledging her presence with a curt nod and a slight twitch of the lips, he walked past her and on to the bedrooms. A few minutes later he returned, frowning slightly, then went back to the dining room, which he'd already seen. At last he looked over, patting the table. "This come with the place?"

Her stomach jumped. "I'd just put it in to stage the house, but…I'm sure we could work something out."

Stroking the beaten-up wood, he half smiled. "Somebody sure put a lot of love into this piece."

"Yeah. He did."

Sharp, steely eyes shot to hers. "You know the artist?"

"Y-yes. He's local. Made the headboard, too."

"Oh, yeah?" Cochran rubbed his chin, then pushed back his leather jacket to slip his hands into his jeans' front pockets. "He does real fine work. What's his name?"

"Eli. Garrett."

Cochran squinted at her for a second, then looked out the dining room's wraparound windows again, to the village below and the snow-flocked Jemez Mountains beyond. Cranky and cynical as Tess felt, even she had to admit it was magical. Then, finally, he turned to her, a look of absolute peace softening his craggy features.

"Sold," he said softly.

Tess's stomach jumped again. "You're ready to make an offer?"

"Oh, we don't need to go through that rigmarole. Whatever they're asking, I'm good." He shrugged. "Makes things easier on everybody."

"That's true, but…wouldn't you like to see a few more properties before you decide?"

One side of his mouth curved up. "You itching to sell me a bigger house?"

"Not at all! It's just…I assumed you'd be used to something more spacious."

Cochran came back into the living room to squat in front of the fire Tess had started in the fireplace before his arrival, rearranging the sputtering logs with a poker like he already lived there. "You know, I grew up in a place probably half this size, with two other kids, my parents *and* my grandparents. Thought the only thing I ever wanted was a house so big I could hear my own echo. Well, I've had a couple of those, and come to find out…it's not all it's cracked up to be."

Straightening, he met her gaze dead-on. "It's just me," he said quietly. "No wife, no kids—" a shadow passed over his face "—so this is plenty big enough for my purposes. So. We got a deal?"

Tess grinned, thinking, *Merry Christmas to me.* "I guess we do. It's getting kind of late now, but we could start the paperwork first thing in the morning?"

"That would be fine."

As they walked out to their respective vehicles, Cochran said, "I've got some loose ends to tie up back in Nashville, so it might be spring before I can move in."

Pulling on her driving gloves, Tess smiled. "Not a problem." Then she paused, her hand on her car's door handle. "Just curious, though…who told you about the house?"

"Guy wouldn't tell me his name," Cochran said from ten feet away, his breath frosting around his face. "Said it didn't matter."

A shiver raced through her that had nothing to do with the cold. "What'd he look like?"

Curiosity flickered in those silvery eyes for a moment before he shrugged. "Tall. Anglo. Curly hair. Maybe ten or so years younger'n me. That's about all I could tell—we were in the Lone Star's parking lot." At her frown, he grinned. "I'd been talking on my cell to my manager, guess a little louder than I'd thought. Afterward this fella approaches me, tells me about the house, then gives me your card. That's all I know. Well," he said, swinging open the door to a spiffy new truck that would make Eli wet himself, "Guess we'll meet up tomorrow then. Nine good for you?"

"Perfect. The address is on the card—the office is right on Main Street. You can't miss it."

With a nod and a half salute, Cash got into his truck and drove off. After Tess slid behind the wheel, however, she simply sat there, gripping the wheel. Her head felt like a snow globe that had just been given a vigorous shake, her whirling thoughts obscuring whatever she was supposed to see.

Fingering the little teardrop, warm against her skin, Tess thought with a wry smile of her emotional barf-fest with her friends the night before. How she knew, without any reservation whatsoever, that she could count on them to be there for her, to listen, to kick her booty when it needed kicking.

That she'd been trusting love all along, even if she hadn't realized it.

That she'd *been* loved all along.

The picturesque scene blurred in front of her as old fears wrestled with the new, tender hope struggling for purchase inside her…a hope she could either nurture, or let shrivel and die.

True, hope had died before, more times than she wanted to count. But never before by *her* hand. Did she really have it in her to simply give up, to let fear win? Was Eli's coming back into her life fate's cruelly taunting her…or offering her another chance at the whole, full-time family she—and her babies—deserved?

She thought of Winnie, daring to take a trip to see the son she'd given up for adoption as a baby, having no idea that journey would lead her to healing, to home, to happiness. Of Thea, giving love one last shot for the sake of not only her unborn son, but for a man who needed her love more than Thea needed to protect her own butt…and finding *her* happily-ever-after in the process.

That trust meant having the courage to take that first scary step, even if you don't know where the hell you're going.

Yanking her car into Reverse, she backed out of the driveway and zoomed back to town to pick the kids up from Carmen's, praying Eli hadn't changed his mind over the past two weeks, that, now that he'd had the chance to think things over, he was really better off without the nutcase that was Tess Montoya.

"Get in, fast, and buckle up!" she called to Miguel, scurrying behind him down Carmen's walkway as Julia and her hippo-size baby bag bounced in her arms.

"Geez, Mom—what's going on?"

"I'm…not sure," she said, strapping the baby in and leaning over to give Micky a kiss on top of his head. "You mind if we stop at Eli's on the way home?"

For a second, the boy's eyes lit up, before wariness smothered the light, and Tess's heart fisted, knowing how many times the little boy had been disappointed.

"I thought you liked Eli," she said softly, cupping his cheek.

He turned away. "He never came back," he said, then looked at her. "He promised he would, but he didn't."

"Oh, baby," she breathed, a thrill shooting through her midsection. "That wasn't his fault. And I'm gonna try to fix it, okay?"

She drank in that dark, trusting gaze for what seemed like an eternity before Micky at last nodded and said, "Okay."

Kid didn't even comment on anyone's Christmas decorations as they drove through the softly swirling snow and past the shop. "Please, please, please be home," she muttered, blowing out a sigh of combined relief and terror when she spotted the old pickup in front of his house. Ten seconds later, they all stood under his tiny portal, Julia swaying and singing in Tess's arms, Micky kicking a ridge of snow off the edge into the yard, Tess closer to throwing up than she'd been since the State Fair incident.

His door swung open. She tried a smile. "Um, hi?"

The look of utter confusion in Eli's eyes slowly, sweetly melted into a combination of hope and tenderness and love unlike anything she'd ever seen in another man's eyes, ever…except, perhaps—in a much less mature form—in Eli's, all those years before.

"Um…hi back?"

"Ho, ho, ho," she said, and he grinned, then leaned over and kissed her. Julia clapped her mittened hands and launched herself into his arms, kissing Eli's cheek. He laughed, then got down on his haunches, Julia balanced against his side.

"Micky?"

Over by the edge of the porch, Miguel turned. Eli held out one arm, whispering, "It's okay, buddy," and the little boy smiled and ran to him, plastering himself against Eli's chest.

Tess smiled, as the last bit of fear melted faster than the snowflakes on her son's curls.

*Just don't do anything stupid,* Eli thought, barely breathing as he watched Tess and Miguel troop into his house. The baby squirmed to get down, then toddled over to Maybelline, sprawled in a lingering patch of late-day sun on his carpet. Julia calmly flopped on her belly, chin in hands, to stare at the cat. The cat in turn lifted bored green eyes to him—*Do I have to make nice to it?*—then seemed to sigh, lifting herself up just enough to bump the little girl's chin.

Micky, on the other hand, made a beeline for the TV. "You got any games an' stuff?"

"That I'd let him play?" Tess said under her breath. Grin-

ning, Eli walked over and pulled out Mario Kart, holding it
up for her approval before setting it up for the kid.

Short people engaged, he turned to Tess. Who crossed her
arms, her head tilted. "I sold the house."

"You did? That's terrif—"

"Why didn't you give Cash Cochran your name?"

Eli walked to the kitchen to check on the pot roast he'd put
in the slow cooker before work. "Because I didn't want it to
look like I was trying to manipulate you."

"Goober," she said softly, and he looked back and grinned
at her. And there it was, in her eyes, her smile, even the way
she was coming closer to peek into the pot:

*Trust.*

"Smells good," she said as relief rushed through Eli's entire
body. "You make it with carrots and potatoes?"

"Is there any other way?"

She smiled, then sat at the table where she could keep an
eye on the baby, who was lying beside the prone cat, sucking
her thumb. Eli replaced the lid, then leaned back against the
counter, waiting. Tess's gaze flitted to his before, laughing
softly, she straightened out a crooked placemat, then tucked
her arms across her ribs. "You must think I'm a couple sand-
wiches short of a picnic."

"No more than the rest of us," Eli said with a shrug, joining
her at the table. "But what I think is that I was expecting too
much of you, too fast. Look, just because I've got visions of
minivans and soccer balls dancing in my head—"

"Really?"

"Really. But…" Glancing away, he blew out a breath, then
met her gaze again. "But I'm fine with slow, if…if you're not
just here to tell me you sold the house."

"I'm not. Just here about the house." She glanced down,
then back up. "Or fine with slow."

"Really?"

She smiled. "Really."

"So all that about autonomy…?"

"There's a difference between being *safe* and being happy. My problem was, I thought they were synonymous."

Eli reached across the table and covered her hand with his. "Who says they can't be?" he said, his chest aching when tears welled in her eyes. Then she lifted their clasped hands to her cheek, kissing his knuckles, and his throat got all clogged up until he finally pushed out, "What made you change your mind?"

Tess half laughed, half sighed. "Lots of stuff. My girlfriends, who now know more about me than my own mother. Which isn't saying much, I realize," she added, shaking her head. "But what finally pushed me over the edge was your eyes. At least, when I finally let myself believe what I saw in them."

"And what was that?"

"A future," she said after a moment. "Something good and sure and, yeah, safe, that's only going to keep growing." Releasing his hand, she fingered the edge of the table, her forehead crunched. "Something, if I'm honest, I never saw in Enrique's eyes. But what did I know? And considering how desperate I was…"

She looked back at him. "I don't need you to define me, or to make me feel worthy. But I do need you, Eli. Make no mistake about it, I need you like I've never needed anyone else, ever. And I *don't* need years or months or even weeks to be sure about that."

Smiling, Eli reached for her hand again, holding it captive in both of his. "Same here," he said, and she laughed. "You know…it takes two to find a balance. If all the weight's on one side of the scale, it doesn't work."

"Yeah," she said. "I think I finally figured that out."

Eli kissed her hand, but didn't let go. "When we were

younger I thought *forever* was the scariest word in the diction-
ary. Now I'm thinking it's the only one that matters. My folks've
been together for more than thirty-five years, and I know for a
fact it hasn't always been easy. But they made a promise to each
other, and they've stuck by that promise no matter what. So I'm
here making that same promise to you and the kids.

"And one more thing," he said, letting go to lean back with
one wrist propped on the table edge. "Just in case I didn't
make this clear enough before? There's nothing sexier on
God's green earth than a woman who knows who she is, what
she wants and how to go about getting it."

"Oh, yeah?"

"Yeah. I got no trouble taking charge if the need arises, but
neither do I feel threatened by a woman asserting herself.
Taking the lead."

The cutest blush ever crept up her neck and across her
cheeks. "Then…you wouldn't have an issue with, say, me
asking you to marry me?"

Eli felt a big grin stretch across his face. "No, ma'am, I
wouldn't have a problem with that at all. C'mere," he said,
motioning for her to sit on his lap. Her own lips tilting in a
smile that promised fun times down the road, she straddled
his thighs and linked her hands at the back of his neck, after
which they kissed each other for a long, long time, until Micky
yelled, "Ew, gross," from across the room.

"You, go back to your game," Eli said, only Miguel said,
"You two gonna get married or what?" and Eli said, smiling
into Tess's eyes, "I think we just might. That okay with you?"

At the sound of sneakers shuffling in their direction, Tess
got off Eli's lap. But Miguel didn't go to her, as Eli might have
expected, but to him, standing with his arms crossed and a
stern expression not unlike those he'd seen on a girlfriend's
father's a time or two before.

"You promise not to make Mama cry?"

"Micky! For heaven's sake—!"

"On my life, buddy."

"And Julia and me can see you every day? You swear you won't go away?"

"Swear," he said, hand on heart.

"Then go for it," the kid said, returning to his game.

"Welcome to parenthood," Tess said, chuckling. Eli pulled her back into his lap.

"Can't imagine anyplace I'd rather be," he said. And her smile, right before she kissed him again?

Best damn moment of his life.

## *Epilogue*

"Five more minutes, Mom, please?"

Hands full of toddler toys, Tess glanced over at the pair of dark eyes barely peeking over the top of the old beige sofa, worn in places, but comfortable as all get-out, sitting in the place of honor in front of the big-screen TV.

"Yeah, c'mon, Mom," Eli said, twisting around to grin at her, his cheek close enough to Micky's to totally block out the Road Runner cartoons on the TV. "It's Friday night!"

"*And* first night of spring break!" Miguel put in, nodding vigorously. "An' anyway, we haven't eaten all the popcorn yet!"

"Oh, well, then," Tess said, dumping the toys in a laundry basket and coming up behind Eli to wrap her arms around his shoulders, her heart melting at the sight of her little boy snuggled tight against his stepdaddy, her daughter already sacked out in her pink fuzzy jammies on his other side. She planted a kiss on Eli's temple, then, suddenly ravenous, reached over to grab a handful of popcorn out of the bowl on his lap. From the center of the coffee table Maybelline opened one eye, sighed and went back to sleep—only to fly off the table when Micky roared with laughter as the Road Runner got the best of poor old Wile E. Coyote yet again.

Chuckling, Eli wrapped his fingers around Tess's left hand and lowered it to his chest, bringing her face close to his. Toying with the slim, diamond-studded band that had been his grandmother's, he whispered, "You should come join us."

"Right. And where would I sit?"

"Hmm," he said, looking from one kid to the other. "You might have a point."

Grinning, Tess gently slapped her husband's chest, then moved around to haul the snoring two-year-old off the sofa to carry her to bed. "One more cartoon," she said warningly to Miguel. "Then it's bedtime, got it?"

"Got it," both man and boy said.

Shaking her head, she carried the little girl down the hall and laid her in her toddler bed. But she'd barely kissed her daughter's cheek and pulled the covers up over her shoulders when she heard the telltale creak of Eli's footsteps in the hall. She looked up in time to see him carry Micky, slumped in sleep with his cheek pressed against Eli's shoulder, into his room across the hall.

Smiling, Tess returned to the kitchen through the hodgepodge living room, feeling a sense of satisfaction in the melding of Eli's and her "stuff" she would have never thought possible. Styles and colors clashed, chairs and tables were squished together in odd arrangements, but she'd never felt more at home.

More at peace.

More…part of something lasting and real and just plain *fun*.

"Hey, you," Eli murmured, coming up behind as she stood

at the sink, rinsing off the dinner dishes. He threaded his arms around her waist and kissed her neck. She shivered; he chuckled. "Getting the kids into their pajamas before we started watching TV was a stroke of genius. You are one brilliant woman."

Smiling, Tess moved his hands to her tummy. "Among other things."

He stilled, then turned her around to face him. "No."

"Yep, O fertile-loined One."

Slowly, a grin stretched across that wonderful, goofy face, before Eli let out a hissed, *"Yes!"* and hugged her. Then kissed her. Then hugged her some more. Then he dropped to his knees to talk to her navel, making her laugh.

"Hey, kid—this is your daddy. So you be good to your mommy while you're in there, okay? And whenever you're ready to come out, I'll be right here, waiting." He pressed a gentle kiss to her belly, then got to his feet to tug Tess to him. "Because I ain't goin' anywhere," he whispered, sealing his promise with a truly *fine* kiss.

And the future beckoned, smiling.

\* \* \* \* \*

**We'll be spotlighting a different series every month throughout 2009 to celebrate our 60th anniversary.**

**Look for Silhouette® Nocturne™ in October!**

Travel through time to experience tales that reach the boundaries of life and death. Bestselling authors Lindsay McKenna, Cindy Dees, P.C. Cast and Merline Lovelace join together in a brand-new, four-book Time Raiders miniseries.

# TIME RAIDERS

August—*The Seeker*
by *USA TODAY* bestselling author Lindsay McKenna

September—*The Slayer* by Cindy Dees

October—*The Avenger*
by *New York Times* bestselling author and coauthor of the House of Night novels P.C. Cast

November—*The Protector*
by *USA TODAY* bestselling author Merline Lovelace

*Available wherever books are sold.*

# nocturne™

*New York Times* **bestselling author
and co-author of the House of Night novels**

# P.C. CAST

makes her stellar debut
in Silhouette® Nocturne™

# THE AVENGER

*Available October wherever books are sold.*

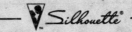

# SPECIAL EDITION

FROM *NEW YORK TIMES*
BESTSELLING AUTHOR

# SUSAN MALLERY

**DESERT ROGUES**

## THE SHEIK AND THE BOUGHT BRIDE

Victoria McCallan works in Prince Kateb's palace.
When Victoria's gambling father is caught cheating
at cards with the prince, Victoria saves her father from
going to jail by being Kateb's mistress for six months.
But the darkly handsome desert sheik isn't as harsh as
Victoria thinks he is, and Kateb finds himself attracted to
his new mistress. But Kateb has already loved and lost
once—is he willing to give love another try?

*Available in October wherever books are sold.*

SSE65481

#1 *New York Times*
bestselling author

# DEBBIE MACOMBER

Dear Reader,

I'm not much of a letter writer. As the sheriff here, I'm used to writing incident reports, not chatty letters. But my daughter, Megan—who'll be making me a grandfather soon—told me I had to do this. So here goes.

I'll tell you straight out that I'd hoped to marry Faith Beckwith (my onetime high school girlfriend) but she ended the relationship last month, even though we're both widowed and available.

However, I've got plenty to keep me occupied, like the unidentified remains found in a cave outside town. And the fact that my friend Judge Olivia Griffin is fighting cancer. And the break-ins at 204 Rosewood Lane—the house Faith happens to be renting from Grace Harding…

If you want to hear more, come on over to my place or to the sheriff's office (if you can stand the stale coffee!).

*Troy Davis*

## 92 Pacific Boulevard

*Available August 25
wherever books are sold!*

MDM2669

www.MIRABooks.com

# REQUEST YOUR FREE BOOKS!

## 2 FREE NOVELS PLUS 2 FREE GIFTS!

# SPECIAL EDITION®

## Life, Love and Family!

**YES!** Please send me 2 FREE Silhouette Special Edition® novels and my 2 FREE gifts (gifts are worth about $10). After receiving them, if I don't wish to receive any more books, I can return the shipping statement marked "cancel." If I don't cancel, I will receive 6 brand-new novels every month and be billed just $4.24 per book in the U.S. or $4.99 per book in Canada. That's a savings of at least 15% off the cover price! It's quite a bargain! Shipping and handling is just 50¢ per book.* I understand that accepting the 2 free books and gifts places me under no obligation to buy anything. I can always return a shipment and cancel at any time. Even if I never buy another book from Silhouette, the two free books and gifts are mine to keep forever.

235 SDN EYN4  335 SDN EYPG

| Name | (PLEASE PRINT) | |
| --- | --- | --- |
| Address | | Apt. # |
| City | State/Prov. | Zip/Postal Code |

Signature (if under 18, a parent or guardian must sign)

### Mail to the **Silhouette Reader Service:**
**IN U.S.A.:** P.O. Box 1867, Buffalo, NY 14240-1867
**IN CANADA:** P.O. Box 609, Fort Erie, Ontario L2A 5X3

Not valid to current subscribers of Silhouette Special Edition books.

### Want to try two free books from another line?
### Call 1-800-873-8635 or visit www.morefreebooks.com.

* Terms and prices subject to change without notice. Prices do not include applicable taxes. Sales tax applicable in N.Y. Canadian residents will be charged applicable provincial taxes and GST. Offer not valid in Quebec. This offer is limited to one order per household. All orders subject to approval. Credit or debit balances in a customer's account(s) may be offset by any other outstanding balance owed by or to the customer. Please allow 4 to 6 weeks for delivery. Offer available while quantities last.

**Your Privacy:** Silhouette is committed to protecting your privacy. Our Privacy Policy is available online at www.eHarlequin.com or upon request from the Reader Service. From time to time we make our lists of customers available to reputable third parties who may have a product or service of interest to you. If you would prefer we not share your name and address, please check here. ☐

SSE09R

# You're invited to join our Tell Harlequin Reader Panel!

By joining our new reader panel you will:

- Receive Harlequin® books—they are FREE and yours to keep with no obligation to purchase anything!
- Participate in fun online surveys
- Exchange opinions and ideas with women just like you
- Have a say in our new book ideas and help us publish the best in women's fiction

*In addition, you will have a chance to win great prizes and receive special gifts! See Web site for details. Some conditions apply. Space is limited.*

To join, visit us at
## www.TellHarlequin.com.

# COMING NEXT MONTH
## Available September 29, 2009

### #1999 THE SHEIK AND THE BOUGHT BRIDE —
**Susan Mallery**
*Famous Families/Desert Rogues*
Prince Kateb intended to teach gold digger Victoria McCallen a lesson—he'd make her his mistress to pay off her dad's gambling debt! Until her true colors as a tender, caring woman raised the stakes—and turned the tables on the smitten sheik!

### #2000 A WEAVER BABY—Allison Leigh
*Men of the Double-C Ranch*
Horse trainer J. D. Clay didn't think she could get pregnant—or that wealthy businessman Jake Forrest could be a loving daddy. But Jake was about to prove her wrong, offering J.D. and their miracle baby a love to last a lifetime.

### #2001 THE NANNY AND ME—Teresa Southwick
*The Nanny Network*
Divorce attorney Blake Decker thought *he* had trust issues—until he met Casey Thomas, the nanny he hired for his orphaned niece. Casey didn't trust men, period. But anything could happen in such close quarters—including an attraction neither could deny or resist!

### #2002 ACCIDENTAL CINDERELLA—
**Nancy Robards Thompson**
Take the island paradise of St. Michel, stir in scandalously sexy celebrity chef Carlos Montigo and voilà, down-on-her-luck TV presenter Lindsay Preston had all the ingredients for a new lease on life. And boy, was Carlos ever a dish….

### #2003 THE TEXAS CEO'S SECRET—Nicole Foster
*The Foleys and the McCords*
With his family's jewelry store empire on the skids, Blake McCord didn't have time to dabble in romance—especially with his brother's former fiancée, Katie Whitcomb-Salgar. Or was the heiress just what the CEO needed to unlock his secret, sensual side?

### #2004 DADDY ON DEMAND—Helen R. Myers
Left to raise twin nieces by himself, millionaire Collin Masters turned to his former—somewhat disgruntled—employee, Sabrina Sinclaire. She had no choice but to accept his job offer, and soon, his offer of love gave "help wanted" a whole new meaning….

SSECNMBPA0909